Praise for
A TAIL AMONG

CW00865478

"In his captivating book, Bill fuses fiction and reality. The storytelling is unique, and the characters spring to life from the pages. Although designed for young-adult readers, these stories are appropriate for all ages."

—DR. MIKE DOW
Psychotherapist, *New York Times* Bestselling Author of *The Brain Fog Fix*, drmikedow.com

"Bill Sheehan has a knack for telling amazing tales within a short story. *A Tail Among Tales* spans decades, and Bill can take you to the 1800s or present day, and you will feel like you're right there with the characters. He has such an amazing way to tell a detailed story."

—DOC JACOBS, HM2, USN (RET.)
Author of *There and Back Again*, Recipient of Bronze Star with Valor and a Purple Heart

"Bill Sheehan's storytelling is captivating and clever. Just when I thought I knew where the storyline was taking me, boom—it turns. This modern-day writer and his gift of painting the picture takes you on a mind-candy journey that will leave you wanting more."

—GABE SPIEGEL
Multi Emmy Award Winner, TV Journalist, 8, Cleveland, Anchor, 12, 4, and 5

"Initially, I thought the book was a mystery, but I was delighted to discover that it was an anthology. Each story had a surprise. Definitely not what it seemed. Bill's book is one of the most enjoyable reading experiences I've had in a long time."

—MICHAEL COMPTON
Entertainment Attorney, Los Angeles

"A feast is in store for all lovers of a good story. Blending fiction with adventure and a smattering of historical facts, Bill Sheehan sets the reader up to ponder and try to guess what is going to happen next. Then he delivers the twist that surprises and delights. Aimed at a young-adult audience, the tales in his latest work hold the attention of individuals of all ages and will have the reader hoping for more."

—KATHLEEN C. ASHTON
PhD, RN, ACNS-BC, CCCTM, Emerita, Rutgers the State University of NJ

A Tail Among Tales

By Bill Sheehan

ISBN 978-1-64663-324-1

Cover design by Skyler Kratofil.

Published by

◤ köehlerbooks™

3705 Shore Drive
Virginia Beach, VA 23455
800–435–4811
www.koehlerbooks.com

A TAIL AMONG TALES

BILL SHEEHAN

VIRGINIA BEACH
CAPE CHARLES

For Kelly,
my most thorough, yet positive, critic and
a constant source of pride and foremost inspiration.

Things are not always what they seem;
the first appearance deceives many;
the intelligence of a few perceives what has been carefully hidden.
—Phaedrus

TABLE OF CONTENTS

THE TAIL OF THE TWISTER

The sun is shining through the beautifully hand-carved wooden horses on the carousel at Paradise Pier. It is a picture perfect day. As the sun's rays hit the various horses, there is an explosion of color throughout the architecture.

Little Joker, a twenty-something-year-old, wearing a red hoodie and Oakley shades, is making his way through the empty ride. He spots Willie, seated on a green bench between some of the horses.

Willie Jett is also twenty-something and has all the characteristics of a beach bum. He wears cutoff jeans, flip-flops, a torn shirt, and sports sandy blond hair, with actual sand in it.

Little Joker sits beside Willie and they begin a discussion. They both look straight ahead. It is unclear what the discussion is about, but after a few minutes they both get up, fist bump, and exit in different directions. There is a small building just in front of the carousel with a ticket office on one side and an administrative office on the other.

The carousel is empty, with no one around except Megan, a summer employee, in the ticket office. She is texting and not paying attention to anything else, her long black hair held back in a sunflower headband and earbuds in.

John Webb and Pearl Hart both approach the ticket office window. There are several small screens showing various locations on the carousel from the security cameras. The pair identify themselves as FBI Special Agents. Webb sticks his shield through the bars of the ticket booth.

"FBI, Miss."

Megan looks up at the Special Agent, "Really?"

Webb takes a quick look at his badge.

"Yes, really. We're looking for a Mr. William Jett, the owner of the carousel."

Megan looks back down at her iPhone, "You mean Willie, the carny that runs this thing?"

Megan points to the office door, barely lifting her eyes from the screen. "He's in there."

Special Agents Webb and Hart put their credentials back into their suit coat pockets and walk towards the door.

As they approach the door, Special Agent Webb puts his right hand back towards his back pocket and rests it on the Glock 22 he has attached to his belt.

Willie answers the door after a couple of knocks. The door swings open to a cluttered office.

Desk full of papers.

A folding chair with a small refrigerator on it in the corner.

An old Army cot with a blanket on one end and an empty pizza box on the other.

"Mr. William Jett?"

"Who wants to know?"

"I'm Special Agent Webb and this is Special Agent Hart, Mr. Jett. We are with the FBI."

Webb and Hart force themselves past the door and into the trashed office.

Special Agent Hart closes the door, "We'd like to come in and talk to you for a few minutes, Mr. Jett."

"You're already in."

Willie gives Special Agent Hart a rather hard look.

"Did I do something wrong, Officer Hart?"

"It's Special Agent Hart. Can we sit down for a few minutes?"

"Yea, sure. Sure."

Willie grabs a sweatshirt from the floor and sweeps it across the seat of two chairs that don't match.

"Sorry for the mess . . . I didn't do anything wrong. What does the FBI want with me?"

There are two diamond rings in a plastic bag lying on the table, which Willie grabs and quickly crams into his pocket.

Special Agent Hart sees the rings, but changes the subject abruptly, "Do you live here, Mr. Jett?"

Willie shifts to a more serious demeanor.

"No, ma'am. But I stay here sometimes. You know, with all the robbers out there these days."

They all sit around a small table, covered in a medley of empty soda cans and beer bottles.

Willie adds quickly, "What's this about, anyway?"

Willie reaches in his pocket and throws the two rings on the table.

"Uh . . . I may deal some hot jewelry from time to time, but that's all." Willie waits for a response.

Willie looks right at Webb.

"Dude, am I gettin busted for this?"

"Mr. Jett, we are working a case in the area and we are going to need to set up surveillance in this office."

"For how long?"

"A couple days. We just need to know that you will cooperate completely with us and not discuss this with anyone."

Willie nods his head. "Sure. Cool. I have nothing to hide . . . but what if I don't cooperate?"

"Obstruction of justice is a federal offence, Mr. Jett, punishable by up to twenty years in a federal prison."

Willie swallows hard.

Special Agents Webb and Hart motion to Willie to step out of the office. They walk out the back door and move toward the carousel.

Special Agent Hart points to the carousel. "There may be more happening on that carousel than kids and tourists having fun."

Willie raises his eyebrows, "Such as?"

Special Agent Webb puts his hands on Willie's shoulder, "We have reason to believe there may be terrorist activity in the area."

"Whoa, dude. So, this is serious."

"Yes, Mr. Jett, very serious. And, we know that there is a firing devise hidden on that carousel somewhere."

"And?"

"And . . . That's where you come in, Mr. Jett."

"So, how can I help?"

Special Agent Webb gets a small notebook out of his pocket and looks at it. "Look, we know he's got it hidden in one of the horses."

Special Agent Hart chimes in, "But there's got to be fifty horses on that thing."

Webb looks at his notebook, "Our intel tells us that it is in the tail of *the Twister*."

Willie's eyes light up.

Webb continues, "What does that mean to you, Mr. Jett?"

"Oh that's easy. All of the horses on the carousel are named after famous racehorses. There's Secretariat and Seabiscuit and a horse called The Twister."

Agent Hart is befuddled.

"The Twister?"

"That's right. The Twister. He's light brown with four white feet. He's really easy to spot because his head is twisted to the right."

Webb puts his notebook back in his pocket, "Then, that's where he's got it. It's hidden in the tail."

A while later, the meeting is over and Willie is walking down the boardwalk with his head down. He looks over both shoulders, approaches the carousel, and walks past Megan in the ticket booth. She is texting and doesn't see Willie.

Willie steps onto the carousel. As he makes his way around the horses, he looks in the direction of the office and doesn't see either one of the agents.

He looks up into one of the surveillance cameras. He steps off the inside of the carousel where the motor and the other controls are.

Matt walks up to Willie on the carousel. Matt is close to Willie's age, wearing a gray shirt with a *Central Amusements* patch across the back and *Matt* sewed over the left breast pocket. He carries a metal toolbox.

"Hey Willie, I'm here to fix the busted stirrup on Man o' War."

Willie's cell phone rings.

"Dude, I gotta take this. Go ahead, you know where he is."

He answers the phone and hurries to get off the carousel.

Willie talks very quietly into the phone, "Dude, what's up?"

He looks in both directions then walks slowly away from the carousel.

"No, I can't tonight. Besides, I can't move hot jewelry when I'm surrounded by cops."

He looks at the lemonade stand and spots a man with binoculars looking at the carousel.

"Oh, Dude, they are everywhere."

He looks over at his office and sees Special Agent Hart peering out the window.

"Never mind, catch you later. Look, I gotta go."

He ends the call and puts the cell phone back in his pocket.

Willie heads back to his office. He enters and sees both agents seated at the small table.

There is a loud knock at the door.

Willie is startled.

He hurries away from the door.

Agent Webb jumps to his feet.

He puts his hand back on his belt as if to draw his firearm.

Agent Hart laughs.

"Relax, relax, I ordered a pizza."

Hart and Webb get out money to pay for the pizza. Hart opens the door.

The pizza delivery boy appears to be confused.

Special Agent Hart looks at her watch, "It's been over an hour. You're two blocks away. How much is it?

"It's six ninety . . . with the delivery."

She hands him some cash.

"Here's seven bucks . . . with the tip."

She takes the pizza and slams the door in his face.

While the feds enjoy their pizza, Willie flops on the cot.

Webb takes a big gulp of his soda.

"Mr. Jett, we're going to need you to help us out tonight."

"Dude, Look, I'm not into being no hero."

"If all goes as planned, you won't have to be a hero, in fact, there's practically no danger at all."

Willie sits up on the edge of the cot, "What do you mean, *practically*?"

Hart stares at Willie, "We'll be there to see that nothing happens."

"Oh, that's very comforting."

Webb interrupts, "Anyway, our intelligence sources tell us that the suspect is going to show up tonight to retrieve the firing device."

Willie does not share Special Agent Webb's excitement. "So, what do I have to do?"

"When we get to the carousel, you will go to the controls and when I give the signal, you turn off the main electrical breaker to the power on the surveillance cameras and the lights."

"Then what?"

"Then, we wait for the perp to show up."

"The perp?"

"Yeah, the bad guy."

Webb gets back to his story.

"He'll go directly to the Twister and when he opens the tail, we will take him into custody."

Willie stands up and heads for the door, "I think I'll pass on this."

"Passing isn't an option, Mr. Jett." Agent Webb takes a big bite of pizza.

Special Agent Hart gives Willie a smirk. "Thanks for volunteering, Mr. Jett."

Night has fallen.

Special Agents Webb and Hart and Willie walk from the office toward the carousel.

The carousel is suspiciously quiet. Not a soul around.

Willie looks back over his shoulder for a quick glance at the lemonade stand.

There is no one there.

Webb, Hart and Willie walk quietly onto the carousel. Willie takes his position by the control panel.

Webb gives a nod to Hart, looks around at Willie and tells him, "Okay, hit the breaker."

There is a click of the circuit breaker.

Everything goes black.

Webb pulls the handcuffs from his belt, and in the moonlight, sees Willie enough to handcuff him to the vertical pole of the horse.

Willie tries to pull away. "Hey, what's this for?"

The circuit breaker click is heard again.

The lights suddenly pop back on.

"Freeze, Barrow!"

There stands Detective Van Wieren from the 23rd Precinct in a rumpled suit and with mussed grey hair, brimming with self-confidence and Detective Kobus, very GQ but aware he is second banana to Van Wieren. They appear out of nowhere.

Webb whips around to find himself looking down the barrel of Van Wieren's handgun. Detective Kobus has a bead on Hart as well.

Webb and Hart both raise their hands slowly.

Detective Van Wieren makes a motion with his gun. "That's right, put those hands up nice and high. You've both done this before, I know."

Then the seasoned detective offers a big smile. "Craig Barrow and Barbara Parker, how long have I been trying to nail you two?"

"We've been watchin' you from the lemonade stand for a couple days now. You know time is always on our side. You just keep your hands up nice and high."

Van Wieren motions to his two uniformed officers, Blake and Peña, to handcuff Barrow and Parker, AKA, Webb and Hart. Willie is totally confused with his arms wrapped around Affirmed's neck, handcuffed to the metal pole coming out of the horse's withers.

"Wait, wait a minute. What about the terrorist?"

Detective Van Wieren gives a hearty laugh.

"Terrorist? Son, there's no terrorist. Mr. Barrow and his friend here are interested in the sixty thousand in cash that's locked up in the tail of the Twister."

Detective Van Wieren uncuffs Willie. "You three follow Detective Kobus to the van."

Willie is still confused, "What do ya mean, three?"

Van Wieren laughs again. "You too, Willie. Crime doesn't pay, son, not even a little crime."

Willie tries to defend himself. "I was just helping the agents."

The two detectives handcuff the three suspects.

Detective Van Wieren gives orders to the two uniformed officers. "Open that tail up, count and bag up the cash, then get it into evidence."

Van Wieren and Kobus escort the three suspects away.

Blake joins Peña by the Twister on the carousel.

Peña opens the door on the tail.

He looks inside with a flashlight.

There is no cash.

Peña looks down in the tail and slowly pulls out a black wig with a sunflower headband on it.

He holds it up to show Blake. He reaches in again and pulls out a gray shirt.

Peña holds it up. It says *Central Amusements* across the back.

Detective Van Wieren escorts the suspects to the police van, mirandizing them as he goes.

"You have the right to remain silent. Anything you say, can and will be used against you . . ."

Twenty or thirty yards behind the detectives are a homeless couple. The man, is ragged and in loose disarray, walking with a limp, using a cane. The bag lady with him is gray and disheveled, slowly pushing a full grocery cart along the boardwalk, the contents of which are covered with an old, blue plastic tarp.

A wad of hundred dollar bills wrapped in a rubber band falls out of the cart onto the boardwalk.

The bag lady hears it drop.

She takes her foot and slowly draws the money near the wheel of the cart.

She gracefully reaches down, picks it up and sticks it in her pocket, as the couple continue their way down the boardwalk.

Author's Note

This story is based on an actual racehorse from an article, "Tales of the Twister," originally printed in *The California Thoroughbred* in 1982, written by Don Walters.

The character, John Webb, was patterned after the real life

lawman, John Joshua Webb, who became an outlaw. According to western folklore, John Joshua Webb was sworn in as a deputy sheriff by Bat Masterson, in Dodge City, Kansas, in 1878. In 1880, Webb was appointed the town marshal of Las Vegas, New Mexico. In the same year, he became a member of the Dodge City Gang, a notorious band of outlaws. He was convicted of murder, broke out of prison, and drifted to Arkansas, where he eventually died of smallpox in 1882.

Pearl Hart, on the other hand, was never a deputy or a sheriff. She led a life of crime and at the age of twenty-eight became a famous outlaw because of her gender. She dressed as a man with short hair and robbed an Arizona stagecoach traveling from Globe to Florence. She was accompanied by her longtime friend, Joe Boot. She was convicted and served time. As legend would have it, she turned up in Globe, Arizona where she was reported to have died in 1955.

Willie Jett, the main character of the story, is based on the infamous William S. Jett. Jett was a private in the 9th Calvary in Virginia. He met David Herold and John Wilkes Booth, who had just assassinated President Lincoln. He escorted them to the Richard H. Garrett tobacco farm in Virginia and he led them into a barn, which Union soldiers would set ablaze to capture Booth.

Craig Barrow and Barbara Parker are in reference to Clyde Barrow and Bonnie Parker, a pair of bank robbers in the 1930s, AKA Bonnie and Clyde.

The Twister was a racehorse in the early 1950s. His registered name was Your Host. He had a twisted head from an injury when he was born. He won many races despite the fact that he was deformed and small. He broke his right front leg in a race in 1951. He was sent to Meadowview Farms in New Jersey where he produced several successful racehorses. He died when he was fifteen in 1961.

FAKE

A white cab pulled up in front of the Eastern Commerce Bank. Three men exited the cab. All three were costumed in black pants, shoes, shirts, and masks. They all had dark glasses. There were two young boys skateboarding by. When they spotted the men, they jumped off their boards and ran behind the payphone on the corner. A lady pushing a stroller saw the men and ran in the opposite direction, pushing the stroller with one hand and trying to dial 911 on her iPhone with the other.

Two of the men chambered a round in their handguns and the third pulled an Uzi out of a canvas bag. They all entered through the heavy glass doors of the bank.

The man with the Uzi fired a barrage of rounds up into the skylight. There were screams and chaos. Falling glass fell all over the white marble floor. One of the cashiers snuck into the back room during the gunfire.

"Alright, nobody move. Do exactly what you are told and no one gets hurt." The man with the Uzi spotted a manager behind his desk. "Okay, you in the suit. Stand up and keep your hand away from that alarm button." He threw the canvas bag in the manager's direction. "Now take that bag and start filling it with cash."

An elderly security guard emerged from the back room with a double-barreled shotgun. He walked up to the man with the Uzi. "Drop it!"

The man with the Uzi pointed his weapon at the guard.

KABOOM! The guard pulled both triggers.

The bad guy was blown against the entrance. Blood was splattered all over the glass doors.

The guard started to reload his shotgun. The other two robbers started to run. They pushed their partner away from the glass doors and headed out of the bank.

The bank guard aimed the shotgun at the man lying on the floor. He gently placed his finger on both triggers again.

"Alright, *cut!*"

The director walked out from behind the camera. She looked around at the scene. She smiled and said, "Nice job, everyone. That's a print. Now let's move in for some close ups."

SILENCIO

A lady of substance in her forties sat quietly on New York's downtown train No. 1. She was on her way to a midtown café for a power lunch with other members of her law firm. She was reading a novel, *The Idiot* by Fyodor Dostoevsky. Her Italian leather purse sat close beside her on the crowded subway bench. The train stopped at the Fifty-Ninth Street station. She was engrossed in her novel, but at the same time lifted her eyes to see if anyone was looking her way, and to see if she had missed her stop.

The conductor's voice was too loud on the over modulated and hissing speaker, "Fiftieth Street next, stand clear of the closing doors."

As the doors closed, a young man with dark glasses and a hoodie squeezed in and took a seat directly across from the lady. She glanced up for a second and then returned to her paperback. The young man sat quietly as the train jerked a bit and then pulled out of the station. The lady couldn't help but look up again as she felt his eyes piercing through those intimidating mirrored lenses. She was feeling a bit uncomfortable as she began to lose track of the paragraph that she had already read about four times. She glanced up quickly and the piercing mirrored lenses seemed to be fixed on her.

The train was crowded, but there was a convenient slash between people standing, through which she could see this miscreant. As the train rumbled its way to the next stop at Fiftieth Street, there were a few restless riders crowding the door in an effort to be one of the first ones off at the next station.

The lady got a small reprieve as a rather rotund man in a cheap wrinkled suit stood in front of her. She was able to take a breath. The train came to a squeaking stop. The doors opened and a gush of human energy filled the door. This time she put her finger in her ear that was closest to the speaker.

"C'mon folks, let em out first. Let em out."

As the people continued to flee the train, the lady put her paperback in her purse and then realized this was her stop as well.

"Next stop Forty-Second Street, Times Square, stand clear of the closing doors."

She panicked.

She jumped up.

She grabbed the vertical steel pole.

She reeled around.

Just as the warning tone was heard, she rushed through the closing doors. The lady was now free of the many deviant deeds she imagined could have happened with the hooded young man and was able to make her way up the crowded steps to the street.

The young man, standing in front of the seat where the lady was seated, flashed a look from one end of the train car to the other. He went to the door. He stood there with his face just a few inches from the glass.

He looked around at the other passengers, all into themselves. But, of course, no one could tell if he was looking at them or not. No one said a word. He needed to exit this train.

Then it happened.

An automated recording.

"We are being held temporarily by the train's dispatcher. We should be moving shortly."

He stood under that loudspeaker but appeared unphased. He was nervous but remained calm.

The doors opened and he bolted. He was free. He raced to the exit and hurdled the turnstile. He headed up the steps, the same steps as the lady just a few moments before.

Up the steps.

Two at a time.

He was out on the street.

He looked around.

No one seemed to be following him, so he stepped forward, looking both ways and checking over his shoulder. Both shoulders.

He headed for the intersection.

He stepped down off the curb to cross.

Bang!

He was hit by a yellow pedicab. The young man grabbed his knee but remained on his feet.

The cabbie stopped, "Dude, you okay?"

The young man nodded his head.

"You sure?"

The young man nodded again. The pedicab pedaled off. The young man lifted the left pant leg of his jeans up to the knee and saw a small trickle of blood, but nothing he hadn't seen before.

He pulled his pant leg back down and looked around.

The sophisticate was browsing through a fashion magazine at a corner newsstand. She handed it to the clerk, "How much is this?"

"It's six dollars."

She reached in her purse to get her wallet and looked up. She spotted the young man on the other corner. She saw the mirrored lenses looking her way again.

"Oh, my God."

She made eye contact with her assailant.

She looked at the clerk.

"Lady, I said it was six dollars."

She threw the magazine back on the pile. "Sorry, I changed my mind."

She took off down the sidewalk, trying to put some distance between herself and the hoodlum with no eyes.

The young man saw her and started to cross the street. He moved with a bit of a limp now and couldn't get up to full speed, but he took off after her.

She was moving pretty quickly in her Anne Klein slingbacks and tight Brooks Brothers suit, but she was determined to get away from this kid.

The chase continued.

The lady reached the corner of Fiftieth Street and 8th Avenue. She looked over her left shoulder and the young man from the train was still in pursuit. She continued down Eighth Avenue not knowing that the young man's injured knee slowed him down.

She reached the corner of Eighth Avenue and Forty-Eighth Street. She spotted a safe haven.

It was the Engine 54 station with the big doors open and fire fighters everywhere. Her pulse slowed a bit as she crossed the walk to enter the station. She smiled invitingly as a couple of the firefighters became aware that she was there. Her next step landed her left Anne Klein heel in the steel grate directly in front of the station. She made a couple of attempts to pull it out. Then, in a panic, she gave it a twist and sheared off the heel. She hopped over and went into the fire station.

The firefighters that saw what happened were all too eager to help her out. One checked the grate for the heel, another offered her a chair, and yet a third offered to look at the shoe.

"Ma'am, you must be in a hell of a hurry."

"Yeah, well, I am a little late for an appointment."

The shaded young man hobbled past the open door of the fire station and continued down Eighth Avenue after his intended mark.

He suspected nothing and saw nothing.

He was focused down the street.

"Here ya go, ma'am." The lieutenant handed her shoe back.

"The heel will have to be glued back on. You'll be able to get by until you can get it fixed. There's a shoe repair right over on Ninth Avenue."

The lady reached into her purse for her wallet. But, before she could find it, the firefighter interrupted her search. "Ah . . . no need ma'am. We were happy to help you out."

She gave an approving nod and thanked the firefighters as she headed for the big open door. The lady cautiously exited the fire station, not knowing that the young man she was running from was now in front of her. She looked around. An aura of calm came over her. She felt safe for the first time since she spotted the young man on the train. She walked with care on her broken shoe as she continued down Eighth Avenue. As she walked, she looked around. She was building her own confidence the longer she was without the trailing young man. But she also used caution by keeping her hand in her right jacket pocket with a firm grip on the small canister of pepper spray that she had carried with her since she moved to New York.

She stopped for the light at the corner of Forty-Seventh Street and Eighth Avenue.

She looked in both directions.

It was a very crowded corner.

A cab was lodged in the crosswalk between scurrying people and another thoughtless cab.

She looked to the right.

Then to the left.

And, there to the left was the young man from the train.

She was two feet away from his face.

His face showed relief.

Her face showed shock.

She could not see his eyes from behind those mirrored lenses.

The lady saw him reach into the front pouch of his hoodie.

She pulled the pepper spray from her pocket.

The young man began to open his mouth as if to speak.

The lady squeezed the trigger on the spray canister.

A direct hit.

The stream of chemicals hit his mirrored lenses.

There was commotion on the sidewalk.

The young man's hands ripped off the shades. He began to wipe at his eyes, which only made the situation worse. He was unsteady in his gate and lowered himself to the sidewalk.

The people on the corner began to dissipate. A man and his wife were watching. "He's probably in a gang. Let's get the hell out of here."

The lady quickly put the pepper spray canister back into her pocket. She saw the young man's face for the first time. She got a good look at all of his features for the police sketch artist.

She noticed a small scar on his right cheek.

The white walk signal began to blink. The man on the corner tugged at his wife as they started to cross the street. "There's never a cop around when you need one."

Three of New York's finest suddenly appeared out of nowhere. A short female sergeant approached the lady.

"Hold it, ma'am."

Officers Hanson and Wayne approached the young man. "C'mon, get up."

They helped him up and quickly turned him against the wall of the building. They did a quick frisk for a weapon.

Hanson turned him back around. "Alright, what's going on here?"

The young man did not answer. He continued to wipe at his eyes as tears streamed down his face.

His mirrored lenses were still lying on the sidewalk.

The sergeant led the lady away from the young man and the chaos that she had just created.

"Thank you, officer. I was being chased by a gang member. He was going to rob me—or worse."

"Did he physically attack you, ma'am, or did you just think he was going to attack you?"

"That young man right there has been chasing me for blocks, ever since I got off the train."

The two male cops heard the lady's response and began to question the young man.

"Why are you chasing this lady?"

The kid did not respond.

"I said, why are you chasing this lady?"

Only silence.

"Alright, you want to do this the hard way?"

Officer Wayne took out his baton and placed it firmly across the kid's back. The young man was now wedged between the officer's baton and the wall of the Starbucks on the corner.

The other cop reached into the kid's back pocket and pulled out a canvas wallet.

The cop looked through it for a minute.

There was a driver's license.

Opposite the compartment where the license was, there were about six business cards.

Officer Hanson removed one and read it.

"Let him go, Jerry."

"What?"

"Yeah, Let him go."

He handed the card to his partner. He read it aloud.

"*Soy mudo y sordo*. I am mute and deaf."

Then, Officer Hanson handed the wallet and the cards back to the young man.

The kid put the wallet in his pocket.

He slowly moved toward the lady from the train.

She stepped closer to the sergeant.

He reached into the front pouch of his hoodie and produced her wallet that had fallen out of her purse on the train bench.

He handed it to her with a smile and a friendly nod.

She was shocked and now she couldn't speak.

He lifted his eyebrows, turned, and limped away.

HIGHBOOTS MCCOY AND EHRICH

New York City, 1888.

"*Stop!* Hold it right there, you two." The boys froze in their tracks. The rotund man in a brown suit grabbed both boys by their shirt collars.

"What do you think you're doing?" He dragged them inside the factory office.

"You two sit here and don't move." Mr. Richter pulled the *Help Wanted* sign from underneath Ehrich's arm and put it back in the window. He pulled up a chair by the two boys as he calmed himself.

"Now, what was that all about?"

"Well, sir" replied Ehrich. "I needed to find some work to help my family out, and I figured if I took the sign out of the window and told everybody in line that I was already hired, they would just all go home and I would get the job."

"What's your name, son?"

"It's . . . uh . . . Ehrich Weiss. What's yours?"

"I'll ask the questions . . . but, if you must know, it's Mr. Richter.

My brothers and I own this factory and we make the finest neckties in all of New York City."

Mr. Richter now focused on the second boy.

"And you. What's your name?"

"Highboots McCoy," he replied with a smirk.

With a raised eyebrow, Mr. Richter asked, "Highboots McCoy? What on earth kind of a name is that? Is that your given name?"

"Nope. My real name is Kelly McCoy. But all my friends call me Highboots, or Boots for short."

"And, just for my satisfaction, how is it that you come by that name?"

"Well, my dad is a horse trainer up at Jerome Park in the Bronx. When I was real little, I used to go there to help him with the horses, and I always wore tall rubber boots to keep my feet dry. "It's just that simple."

Mr. Richter pondered for a moment.

"Okay, I'm going to tell you two how simple it's going to be. I'm going to call Sergeant Halinan over at the precinct and have him take you two back to your folks. Where do you boys live?"

Ehrich stood up in protest, "But I really did come here for a job. I'm a really good worker, and like I said before, my family really needs the money."

Mr. Richter now had a very sour look on his face. Ehrich saw this opportunity slipping away and responded respectfully, "I live at two-two-seven East Seventy-Fifth Street, sir, and Boots lives around the corner. . . and . . . uh . . . I could start work tomorrow."

Mr. Richter paused for a moment. He stared at Ehrich.

"Alright, I'm going to go back on my own word just this once. You be here at seven tomorrow morning, and we'll see how good of a worker you really are. Agreed?"

"Yes, sir. I'll be here and ready to make the best ties ever. C'mon, Boots."

The boys left the store and waved very courteously to Mr. Richter.

They headed up Broadway for the Upper East Side. They jumped on the back of one of those new electric street cars. There were more places to hide on them than on the older horse-drawn ones.

Although they were fourteen, the boys were both pretty small for their ages and they were able to slide into a seat near the rear of the car without the conductor seeing them.

"Want to see a trick?" Ehrich reached into his pants pocket and pulled out a nice, shiny new quarter. Boots stared at it as a ray of sunshine hit it and reflected up into his eyes.

"Hey, that's a quarter! Where'd you get that?"

"I've had it for a while. Would you like to see it disappear?"

"You mean like magically disappear?"

"Yeah," Ehrich said very confidently.

"Sure, if you think you can." Boots watched intently as Ehrich placed the quarter in his right hand, closed it, then passed his left hand over his right as if magic was really going to happen. He turned the right hand palm down and very slowly opened it until all of the fingers were spread well apart. Boots' eyes were now as big as half dollars. Ehrich continued by turning the right hand over and showing the empty palm to an amazed Boots.

"It's gone. You really did make it disappear. How did you do that?" Boots begged him. "C'mon, tell me how you did that."

Ehrich gave Boots a bit of a smirk and raised his eyebrows quickly. "It's magic. Besides, a magician never tells how things are done."

Boots was not convinced that Ehrich was really a magician.

"Oh yeah? Well, I'd like to know what happened to that quarter!"

Ehrich smiled at his friend.

"Look in your right coat pocket."

"What?" said Boots as he reached in his pocket, pulling out that shiny new quarter. "Well, I've got some magic for you. How you going to get it back?" Without warning Boots jumped off the streetcar and headed off running with the shiny coin still in his hand, waving it around to taunt Ehrich.

"Gimme that back, Boots!" Ehrich was now off the streetcar as well, chasing Boots up Sixth Avenue.

Boots McCoy and Ehrich Weiss had been friends for about a year or so. They lived on the same block, and one day they just started talking and realized that they were both born on the same day—April 6, 1874. When they were together, they were inseparable, but when they weren't, they had very separate and different lives.

They were both a bit thin and scrawny, tough as prairie birds, and always on the go. They both came from very poor families and they had both worked since they were young to bring in money to help their families.

There was never any discussion or thought about keeping the money they earned for themselves. They were both very serious young boys; neither of them spent much time playing traditional games or practicing tomfoolery.

Ehrich Weiss came from Appleton, Wisconsin, the son of a Jewish Rabbi and teacher. Rabbi Weiss ran a Hebrew school for a while. He and Ehrich were living in Mrs. Leffler's boarding house on East Seventy-Ninth Street until they were able to earn enough money to afford the flat where they were now living. He read a lot—a lot about magic, anyway—and he worked a lot. He had many jobs, anything to help bring money in.

He liked Boots a lot. They seemed to have this common bond of independence and energy. Their understanding for each other was more mindful than anything else. They didn't discuss their relationship. They just understood it.

Boots hailed from a small railroad town in Ohio, called Crestline. It was the hub of the state in the 1880s. That's where the Pennsylvania Railroad and the Cleveland, Cincinnati, and Chicago Railroad lines crossed. Boots knew a lot about the trains in Crestline. He spent a lot of time around the ticket office in the center of town.

His father trained horses on a farm just north of town. Then they would ship the horses on the trains, usually to New York, to the big tracks for racing.

He liked to spend time looking at the pictures inside the station. There was a picture of President Lincoln standing on the train platform. He really couldn't explain the allure of the picture, but he spent lots of time enjoying it. And there was a bigger picture right beside it, another picture of Lincoln. It was the president's funeral train. It stopped in Crestline to refuel on the night of April 29, 1865, some nine years before Boots was even born.

The locomotive that pulled it was named The Nashville. The Nashville was huge in the picture, with steam coming out down by the wheels. Boots used to look at that picture for what seemed like hours wondering what it would feel like to ride on a train like that with all that power.

He knew about power, horsepower. Being small in size, he was able to work for his father as an exercise rider on the horses. That saved money as well. That was one less person his father had to hire. Mr. McCoy soon realized that he needed to be more involved in the training process, so one day he and Boots packed a suitcase each and got on the same train as the horses they were shipping to New York. They got lost on their first trip to the big city and ended up in front of a small apartment building on East Seventh-Sixth Street. And, that's where Boots met Ehrich. Boots also read a lot. He would play hooky from school every chance he got, but he liked to read. He spent a lot of time in the barns looking through the American Veterinary Review, a professional journal that most of the horse doctors had with them from time to time.

He understood a lot of the information, and what he didn't understand by reading, he would quiz the veterinarians about when they came to the barns to make their calls. Just by standing around watching and listening he also learned a great deal about horseshoeing and racing.

Boots and his friend Ehrich were going through a growth spurt at this time and Boots realized that because of his growing size he would not be able to race the horses. He was already taller than some of the jockeys. He was satisfied with just exercising them in the mornings and taking good care of them in the evening.

He was very excited about learning about the medical problems they had and how to fix them. He actually thought about going to a veterinary college someday. That is, if he could ever get through his present school.

Boots and Ehrich were on their way home one day from some errands in midtown and they ended up on the stoop at Ehrich's flat on Seventh-Sixth Street.

They sat quietly for a while just reflecting on the day.

"You mad at me or something?"

Boots was a bit surprised at that question. "No, Ehrich. Why would I be mad at you?"

"You just been acting a little funny lately, that's all . . . kinda quiet and all."

In an instant Boots came to life, "You know what I saw the other day?"

Ehrich threw a few stones into the street. "No, what?"

"I saw a foal get born."

Ehrich's eyes widened and his mouth flew open, "You saw a what?"

"A foal. You know, a baby horse."

"Did you throw up?" Ehrich snickered.

"No, I didn't throw up . . . I mean, well, there was some blood and . . . well . . . other stuff, but actually it was pretty exciting."

Ehrich just sat there listening to this story.

"The mare just laid down and groaned a little bit and out came this little horse, all wet and shaky. Me and Pop wiped it off with some feed sacks and then he stood up in about ten minutes. It was pretty amazing."

Ehrich was a bit amazed himself. "You like that sort of thing? I mean you talk about it all the time."

"Yea, about as much as you talk about magic." Boots got back to his story. "I really like working with the horses and helping the vets when they come to the barns. I might try to go to a vet college someday."

Then Ehrich got back to the original question. "So, that's the reason you been mopin around?"

"No, that ain't the reason."

"Well, what is it, then?"

A long pause that seemed to last forever passed as Boots took a moment to muster the energy for his big announcement.

"Pop found a place in the Bronx to live . . . we have to move."

"Why?"

"Pop says it's a lot closer to the track, and it's a bit cheaper for him."

"So, when is this going to happen, Boots?"

"The beginning of next month, I guess."

"That's in two weeks."

The two friends just stared at one another for a while.

They both wondered what to say next.

Ehrich broke the ice, "Well, I've never been up to Jerome Park before. This will force me to come up to the track and see what it's all about."

Boots had his head down and responded quietly, "We'll probably never see each other again."

"Don't be stupid . . . of course we will."

"Yeah? . . . when?"

Ehrich, the more optimistic of the two, smiled. "Look, I can come up there and you can come down here. Ya know, it's only a few miles. We're only a train ride away."

For some reason Boots was not entirely convinced. "Oh yeah, guess what I called him?"

Ehrich was puzzled, "Who?"

"The foal, that's who."

"I couldn't guess."

"The Nashville."

Suffice it to say that Boots did indeed move uptown with his dad. And, over the next three years he and his good friend Ehrich saw very little of each other. Ehrich made it up to the track a few times and Boots came down to the Upper East Side once or twice, but they never had the time to have one of their good discussions like they had when they were neighbors.

Their meetings were brief and, like the young businessmen that they were, they usually discussed their work. Ehrich was all about magic and Boots talked about the horseracing business.

One summer morning they were both sitting on Ehrich's stoop as they had so many times before. They were both seventeen now and neither had actually grown much over the last three years.

This meeting would have particular significance.

It would be the last time that they would ever see each other.

They both took turns telling stories and telling about their futures, then Boots stood up and said, "Well, Ehrich, I got to get back up to the park. Since I started training for my dad, I've had even less time to do anything but work at the track. Maybe someday I'll be a famous horse doctor. You can read about me in the paper."

Ehrich looked Boots right in the eye, "And I'm going to be the most famous magician in the world, and you will definitely be reading about me someday."

Boots extended his hand to his friend and they both enjoyed a heartfelt clasp.

It lasted several seconds.

They released their hands and both looked away.

Boots turned to walk away and suddenly stopped in his tracks. He turned toward Ehrich, who hadn't moved.

He gave a big reassuring smile and said, "Bye, Ehrich . . . I certainly hope you know what you're doing."

He did. Later that same year Ehrich Weiss changed his name and became known as Harry Houdini.

Author's Note

Harry Houdini's birth name was Ehrich Weiss and he was the son of a rabbi from Appleton, Wisconsin. He was born in Hungary on March 24, 1874, but he always listed his birthday as April 6, 1874.

The help wanted sign in the window was an actual event in young Ehrich's life. In real life, he became an assistant cutter in H. Richter's Tie Factory in New York.

He really lived with his father at Mrs. Leffler's Boarding house on East Seventy-Ninth Street in New York. And, at the age of seventeen, after reading the memoirs of the French magician, Jean-Eugene Robert-Houdin, he did indeed change his name to Harry Houdini.

The little town in Ohio, Crestline, where Boots McCoy hailed is still considered a railroad community, although the passenger trains no longer stop there and the famous roundhouse was dismantled in 2007. There is controversy over whether Lincoln really stood on the train platform, but there is evidence to show that his funeral train stopped in Crestline for refueling on April 29, 1865.

The Jerome Park racetrack existed and was the site of the first Belmont Stakes in 1867.

The Nashville also existed—the locomotive, but not the horse.

The *American Veterinary Review* was first published in 1877. It ran until 1900, when Dr. Alexandre Liautard changed it to the *Journal of the American Veterinary Medical Association*.

Kelly "Highboots" McCoy was a fictional character and his relationship with Ehrich Weiss was also made up for this story.

THE BOGOTA CROSSING

Chapter 1

"Hey, Rolo! Some dude in a suit is here to see you."

Pablo Morales steps from the shower room, wraps a towel around his waist, and shakes his long black hair like a dog just after a bath.

"Who is it?"

"I don't know. Says it personal. Probably from the bank. Came to get his credit card back.

"Real funny, Tony. Where is he?"

"Coach's office."

A few minutes later, Pablo appears in Coach Hutson's office in shorts and a blue-and-red striped soccer jersey with the number ten and *Messi* printed on the back.

"Coach, did you want to see me?"

"No, Rolo, I don't, but Mr. Bartels here does."

"Is there something wrong, Coach?"

Coach Hutson smiles at Pablo and extends the smile to Mr. Bartels. "This is Pablo Morales, Jake."

Jake Bartels extends his hand to Pablo and introduces himself. "Jake Bartels, Pablo. I represent the Manhattan Booters in Major League Soccer. Coach Hutson was kind enough to let us use his office for a little while. I'd like to talk to you about soccer."

Coach Hutson walks toward the door.

"Look, you two have a lot to talk about, Jake. Take all the time you need. I'll be outside if you need me."

Pablo shakes his head as if he were waking from a dream as the coach exits the office.

"Sit down, Pablo."

Jake sits in the coach's desk chair, and Pablo slowly lowers his slight five-foot, seven-inch, 120-pound frame into the leather couch.

"Is Rolo your middle name?"

"No, it's a common nickname for someone from Bogota. Most of the guys on the team call me Rolo."

Jake gets right to business. "Pablo, I'll get right to the point. Are you aware of the Manhattan Booters soccer team?"

"Uh, yes, sir, I am aware."

"Well, I'm a scout and player advisor for the Booters, and I have been assigned to observe you and another player on this team for almost a year now."

Pablo leans forward on the couch. "You've been watching me play for a year? And I didn't even know about it?"

"That's right, Pablo. I try to stay undetected for as long as I need to. I wouldn't want to unduly influence your playing skills."

"Wow, that's crazy. I didn't even know about it."

"You weren't supposed to know about it."

Pablo sits back in the leather couch again. "Can I ask who the other player is?"

"Well, you can ask, but I can't disclose the name. That's not important right now."

"Okay."

"What is important, Pablo, is that our franchise has become interested enough in you to offer you a chance to try out for the Booters, which may lead to a contract with the MLS."

Pablo offers a huge smile. "No, way."

"Yes, way." Jake lets that sink in for a moment. "But I need a lot more information about you, and of course, I'll want to talk to your parents."

"Yeah, but I'm eighteen now."

"I know, Pablo. But I need to get some basic background information and history before we can bring you on board."

Pablo knows why. "You mean, you have to check to see if I'm legal or not."

"Yes, among other things."

Pablo gives a big sigh.

Jake continues, "I can tell you that I have had several discussions with your coach already, and he gives you a very positive recommendation. He tells me you really excelled in the youth leagues you played in back in Colombia. He also says you carried a very good grade point in high school and you graduated just last week in the top 10 percent of your class.

"You mean Coach Hutson knew all this time?"

"Yes, Pablo, he did."

Pablo shakes his head. "And he never said a word."

"So when would be a good time to meet your parents?"

"Well, Mr. Bartels, my mom works a lot, and it would be hard to find a time when she's around."

Jake is relentless. "And your father, when can we talk with him, then?"

"Well, he is still in Colombia."

"Pablo, talking with your parents is not negotiable." Jake gets up and moves to Pablo. Pablo rises. Jake hands Pablo a business card and offers him a handshake.

"You are an extremely talented player, but MLS is also a business, and we have to cover all of our bases. When you are ready to meet me again—with your parents—give me a call. I wouldn't wait too long." Jake pauses. "Do you understand, Pablo?"

Pablo swallows hard and looks down at the business card.

"Yes, sir. I understand."

Jake opens the door to Coach Hutson's office. He stares at Pablo's jersey for a moment. "I see you are a Messi fan."

"Oh, yeah. I only wish I had moves like that guy."

"You do . . . Pablo, Rolo, Morales."

Pablo beams with pride. "Thanks a lot for meeting with me, Mr. Bartels."

"It was a pleasure to meet you, Pablo."

Jake exits the office, and as Pablo watches him go, he sees Coach Hutson looking back at him with a convincing smile and an undeniable confidence.

"Coach, I can't believe this is happening."

"Believe it, Rolo. It's happening. See you tomorrow at practice."

Pablo shoulders his backpack and stops just outside the coach's office to see his ten-year-old brother, Tino, leaning against the wall with his arms folded.

"Finally."

"Hey, little bro, sup? I had to meet with this guy for a little while."

"Who cares? What are you making me for dinner?"

"How about your favorite, *carne asada* and *yucca*?"

A fist pump. "Yes!"

He jumps to give his big brother a high-five. Pablo puts his arm around Tino, and they disappear down the hallway.

Chapter 2

The church bells are ringing on this beautiful, hot Sunday morning in College Point, Queens. Jake Bartels' XJ6 looks a bit out of place parked in front of the little Seventh Avenue apartment. As Jake approaches the door, a Chihuahua begins to bark, and Tino walks toward the door.

"Hi, is this the Morales residence?"

"Who are you?"

Jake tries to look through the battered screen. "I'm Jake Bartels. I'm looking for Pablo Morales. Does he live here?" Jake can barely hear anything with the dog's incessant barking.

Andrea Santiago comes to the door. "*Quien es?*"

Now, Jake can't hear and can't understand a word.

"Tino, *lleva el perro a la cocina.*"

"Okay, okay." Tino picks up the dog and takes her into the kitchen.

"I'm looking for Pablo Morales," Jake repeats.

Andrea opens the door and motions for Jake to come in. "Oh, yes, Pablo, Pablo. Come in. Come in."

Tino reenters the living room. Jake sits in a rather rickety chair that wobbles. Andrea heads for the kitchen.

"Hi, I'm Tino, Pablo's brother."

"Tino Morales?"

"No, Tino Santiago."

Jake shakes his head a bit but continues, "I was supposed to meet Pablo here for a meeting with him and your mom."

"He just ran down to the Latin Bakery on Main Street. He should be back any minute. Oh, yeah, sorry about the door, but I'm not supposed to let in any strangers."

"Well, Tino, that's a good rule to follow. Say, do you think we could talk for a few minutes with your mom until Pablo gets back?"

Tino thinks for a minute. "Not really. See, Jake? Can I call you Jake?"

Jake is forced to laugh, clearly enjoying meeting young Tino. "Sure." Another laugh.

"See, Jake. Mom doesn't speak much English, and I don't speak much Spanish. We sort of rely on Pablo to translate for us."

"How do you all communicate?"

"I don't know, but we seem to get by. Pablo and Nina, that's our Chihuahua, are the only two that are really bilingual."

"How old are you?"

"Ten."

"You don't act ten." Jake is still amused that Tino asked to call him by his first name. "Anyway . . . "

Jake is relieved to hear Pablo's footsteps coming up the steps. Pablo comes in and hands Tino the grocery bag. He motions to the kitchen with his head, and Tino complies without speaking.

Pablo turns his attention to Jake. "I see you've met Tino."

"Yeah. That kid is a trip."

"Yes, sir, he can be a bit of a handful at times, but he's my biggest fan. I don't think he's ever missed one of my games in the last two years. One time, I even snuck him on the bus when we played in Jersey. Coach was really ticked off, and Mami grounded me for a week. But we sure had fun. Mami works every evening, so I cook Tino dinner, and I sorta guilt him into coming to my games. I think he really enjoys coming, though."

Andrea enters with a glass of iced tea for Jake. He takes it and looks at it for a moment.

Pablo sees him examining the glass. "It's okay, Mr. Bartels. It's just Snapple."

Pablo motions for Andrea to sit. *"Mami, por favor, sientate con nosotros. El Sr. Bartels quiere hablar con nosotros."* Pablo turns to Jake. "I asked her to join us and talk with us."

Jake opens up a leather portfolio and pulls out a few papers. Tino has re-entered the living room and sits on the arm of Jake's chair, looking over his shoulder at the forms.

"I have some questions for you today, Pablo, and then I will leave some forms that need to be filled out. Like I said in Coach's office, the franchise wants to cover all of their bases.

Tino pipes up, "Jake, you could at least use a soccer cliché."

Jake gives a smile. Pablo gives a firm look at Tino over the top of his glasses. *"Constantino!"*

Tino feels the heat. "He always calls me that when he's angry at me. I better go in my room and work on level three.

Jake gets back to business. "So, Pablo, I will need your resident status and your birth certificate to start, then a transcript from your high school."

Pablo looks at his mom. *"Quiere ver mi certificado de nacimiento."*

Andrea looks back to Pablo with a very concerned stare.

Pablo looks back at Jake. "Uh, well, Mr. Bartels, uh, that might take some time. See, we don't have any copies, plus I'm not sure where it is."

"Well, Pablo, if you give it to me, I'll take it back to the office and have a few copies made."

"I guess that would be okay."

"*Mami, por favor, Traeme el certificado de nacimiento.*" Andrea leaves the room to get the document. Pablo looks back to Jake. "Mom will bring it right out."

"And, Pablo, I have to ask, how is it that you are Morales and your mom and Tino are Santiago?"

"Uh, Morales is my father's name. Jack Morales. He and my mom split up right after I was born. It's all on the birth certificate."

"Okay. Good to know."

Jake is not convinced that he has heard the truth, having seen the concern on Andrea's face and the hesitation in Pablo's voice.

"The paperwork always takes a little time, but in the meantime, we need to get you scheduled for a tryout. Pablo, up to now, soccer has just been fun, but this will be the most important soccer game you will play. It'll take place over in Jersey at our training facility. You'll be playing against other current academy team members.

"I'm totally stoked, Mr. Bartels."

"Don't forget, just to put it in perspective, every player on the field will be a Pablo Morales or even better."

"Yes, sir. I'll be ready."

Andrea walks in the living room and hands an envelope to Pablo, who in turn hands it to Jake. He looks at it briefly and puts it in his portfolio.

"Okay then."

Jake heads for the door. "Thanks for your time. We will be in touch, and get ready for the tryouts, Pablo."

Jake offers a sturdy handshake to Pablo and Andrea and pushes open the screen door.

A voice from the back room says, "See ya, Jake."

Jake laughs and shakes his head going down the steps to the sidewalk. Quietly, so only Pablo and Andrea can hear, he says, "See ya, Tino."

Chapter 3

"Goooaaalll!" Tony yells at the top of his lungs, pulls his jersey off while running to midfield, and throws it at Pablo. Pablo stands there, holding it without any of the celebration, with a disgusted look on his face. He holds up the jersey like a matador, and when Tony circles around him, Pablo throws it over Tony's head. "I don't think you need to practice that as much as you do scoring."

"Hey, I'm just getting in winning mode. And what's with you these last few days? Look, we all know there's been an MLS scout hangin' around here the last few weeks."

"That's right, Tony, and this might be my only shot at makin' it to the MLS, and I'm not going to blow it. I'm as serious as I have ever been about soccer."

"Dude, you're takin' all the fun out of it."

"Tony, it will be a lot more fun if I make one of the teams."

They both head for the locker room. Tony and Pablo are the last ones off the field after practice. Tony stops. He grabs Pablo's arm and says, "Hey, Rolo. Wait a minute."

"What's up?"

"Did you talk to Jake Bartels yet?"

"Who?"

"You know who."

"I don't know what you're talking about."

"Hey, Pablo. It's me, Tony, remember? Look, can I be honest with you?"

Pablo looks concerned but doesn't answer.

"We all know Bartels came here to pick two players to try out for the Manhattan Booters. He picked me, and we also know that you're by far the best player on the team, with no current plans to go to college."

"So?"

"So if he picked me, then he must have picked you."

Pablo grabs Tony by the arm and leads him over to the corner of the bleachers where he knows no one will see or hear them. He looks around to be sure they are alone.

"Tony, you shouldn't be talking about any of this. Whoever gets picked is supposed to keep it quiet."

"Yeah, so did he talk to you yet?"

Pablo looks around again, and after a long pause, he says, "Yes, he came to my house and talked to me and my mom. Wanted to talk to my dad too."

Tony offers a huge smile. "Dude, this is the bomb. I've never been so stoked in all my life. To think I might actually make it to the MLS."

Pablo returns the excitement, but then, he is back to reality. "Tony, there's a long way to go. First, you gotta get through the tryouts, which is going to be brutal. Then, you gotta do all the admin stuff, you know, paperwork and interviews, and then you actually have to get picked for the team.

"Do you think we could be roommates when we go to out-of-town games?"

"Tony, you're livin' in a dream world. Get serious."

"I am serious, Rolo. We graduated from this school over a month ago, and we have both been here every day since then practicing.

"I want to stay fit, Tony. You know, keep in shape?"

"And I also bet you know why."

"What are you talkin' about?"

"Come on, Rolo. Don't tell me you don't know."

"No, Tony, honestly, I don't know."

"Well, I didn't know either until I overheard Coach and Bartels talking in Coach's office about it."

"About what?"

"They're only going to pick one."

Chapter 4

Tony and Pablo walk out on the field together, a beautiful field with real grass, manicured beyond anything they both have ever seen before. They both wear plain bright yellow jerseys, Booter's shorts, and socks given to them by the equipment manager, and their own beat-up soccer shoes leftover from high school. They go over to the sideline and wait for Coach Miller to get them started.

Coach Miller walks over to the boys and gets right down to business. "Okay, fellas, being the professionals that you aspire to be, I would gather that you have taken the time to get warmed up and are ready to work." They both nod, but of course, neither have warmed up. Coach Miller continues, "Morales, let's see what you do at midfield. I'm told that you're proficient with both legs, so take the middle position. I need you to feed Drago about two or three passes and, Drago, I want to see your best dribbling, pass through the defense, and score."

Tony swallows hard, then looks at Pablo. Pablo shakes his head, acknowledging the direction that he has been given.

"This is the chance you've been waiting your whole life for, boys. Don't hold back. Give me 100 percent. Understand me?"

Pablo is a little anxious, but he speaks right up, "Yes, Coach, we understand."

"You, Drago?"

"Sir?"

"Drago, do you understand?"

Tony looks as though he doesn't understand the question. "Uh, yes. Uh, yes, Coach."

"All right, fellas, let's see what you got."

The boys take their places among the other players on the field. The offense is wearing white jerseys and the defense is wearing blue jerseys. One of the players with a white jersey and the ball approaches Pablo. "I'm Adam Cole."

Pablo recognizes the name from seeing Adam on television, realizes where he actually is, and gives a little smile.

"Morales, right?" Adam asks him.

"Yes, sir."

"You don't have to call me sir."

"Okay."

"Now, you and I will make a couple of passes. When we get close to the penalty area, you feed Drago, and hopefully, he scores."

Pablo nods his head.

Adam drops the ball, passes it over to Pablo, and Pablo starts down the field. Using his special gift for footwork, Pablo figure eights around a blue shirt, sees Tony in the clear, and passes. Tony, about twenty feet from the net, kicks it hard. It not only sails over the net but lands in the third row of the stands.

Coach Miller, who is watching carefully, shakes his head. "Well, he's got plenty of leg, I'll say that for him. Maybe he just needs glasses."

One of the equipment managers retrieves the ball and passes it back out to Adam.

Adam sets up to go again. He waits for Coach Miller's signal.

"Okay, Drago, let's go again. Hey, relax, huh?"

Adam drops the ball, passes to ball to Pablo, and Pablo works it past a couple of defensemen, in hopes of getting Tony closer to the net this time.

Again, Pablo makes a nice, clean pass to Tony. Tony kicks it with all his might. The ball hits the upright post on the goal, bounces back, and hits a defenseman in the back of the head. Coach blows his whistle.

Tony looks at Pablo and gives a big shoulder shrug. Pablo gives Tony a thumbs-up and quietly says, "C'mon, Tony. You can do this."

Coach Miller looks at one of the assistant coaches. "Well, at least he's getting it closer to the net." He looks out at the field. "All right, again."

Adam drops the ball a third time. Adam passes it to Pablo, and Pablo works the ball even closer to the net and closer to Tony. Tony has a nice clear shot. He works the ball back and forth between feet, dribbles it around a defenseman, and winds up to score.

Pablo manages a smile, and to himself, he says, "C'mon, Tony."

This time, Tony kicks it with a little less enthusiasm, right into the arms of the goalie. The whistle blows.

"Okay, Morales. You're up. The objective here, fellas, is to actually get the ball into the net."

"Yes, Coach."

Tony and Pablo exchange places. As they pass each other on the field, Tony says, "I blew it, Rolo. No way they're going to keep me after that pitiful display." Tony sees Adam. He extends a hand. "Hi, I'm Tony Drago."

"Yeah, Adam Cole."

"Yeah, I know Mr. Cole. I see you on TV all the time."

Adam takes the ball and drops it on the ground. "You can call me Adam. C'mon, Drago, let's just play soccer."

Adam passes the ball to Tony much the same as he passed it to Pablo. Tony dribbles past a couple of defensemen and sees Pablo in the clear. Instead of passing, he tries to display a little fancy footwork. He barely gets it past a third defenseman and, in desperation, offers a sloppy pass to his friend. Pablo has to outmaneuver a big defenseman for the ball. He manages to get it away from him and heads for the goal. His dribbling is impressing Coach Miller, who is watching from the sidelines. "This kid has definitely got some moves."

Pablo enters the penalty area. The goalie is fixed on Pablo. Pablo looks right, moves right. The goalie commits. Pablo taps the ball past the goalie on the left and into the net.

"Okay, Morales, let's see that left foot, now."

Coach Miller moves onto the field to get a closer look at this little guy in action. "Reset, Adam."

Adam Cole has the ball and is about to drop it again.

"Okay, Drago, stay on the right side this time and feed him the ball across the field."

Tony takes the pass from Adam and is dribbling with a bit of difficulty due to his anxiety, not to mention two rather robust defensemen in his path. Pablo closes in on the trio, steals the ball, and scores with his left foot from just outside the penalty area.

"Nice job, Morales." Coach Miller is pleased, and he walks out onto the field to talk to Morales.

Tony feels the tension and approaches the coach. "Sorry, Coach. I couldn't get around the defenders."

"That's Okay, Drago, I saw what I needed to."

Coach Miller turns his attention to Adam and Pablo. "All right, Adam, feed one in the air to Morales and let's see what he can do with a header."

"Cool, Coach. Will do."

Adam and another offender dribble the ball toward the goal. Pablo finds a good position right in the center of the penalty area.

Adam sees him in the clear and kicks the ball high in the air. It is a perfect kick. Pablo sees it coming and jumps. He is airborne and is just about to connect with the ball and—

Bang! His legs are both hit. He feels his knees buckle. He looks down to see the grass coming up to meet his face. He braces for impact. He lands on his left shoulder and left hip.

He is in immediate pain.

A lot of pain.

Pain he has never felt before.

He grabs his left shoulder with his right hand.

He can't move.

He looks up to see fuzzy soccer players. He can barely make out Adam's face. And Tony is there also.

"C'mon, fellas, give him some air." Coach's more than ample voice is heard across the field. The rest of the team gathers around. The trainer is there in a flash.

"Lay still, Morales. Where is the pain?"

"My neck and my shoulder."

"Okay, roll over on your back real slowly. I'll help you."

"Holy, crap!" Pablo pulls back a bloody right hand to reveal his left collarbone sticking out through the skin.

"Stay real still, Morales. You're going to be okay."

The trainer takes some gauze pads out of a package and gently places them over the end of the bone. He pulls Pablo's left arm over his belly. "Let's get him on the cart."

The trainer and his staff get Pablo on the cart and on his way to the locker room.

Coach Miller looks at the assembled crowd. "All right, guys. That's all for today. Hit the showers, but give Doc enough space to work on Morales, okay?"

Tony looks concerned. "Is he going to be all right, Coach?"

"Yea, most likely. But he won't be playing for a while."

Tony nods. "Yeah."

"We'll know more when we look at the tape."

"Tape? What tape?"

"We work at the professional level here, Drago. We videotape all practices."

Chapter 5

Tino sits on his brother's hospital bed. He and Pablo are looking at an x-ray.

"See this, little bro?" Pablo points to the x-ray of his collarbone. "That's a fractured clavicle, and that is a steel plate on the outside of the bone. See the screws in the plate?"

"Yeah. That's pretty cool."

"You think so?"

"Yeah."

"Well, I got to keep that plate on for a while 'til the bone heals. It was broken in two different places."

"Can you play soccer, again?"

"Of course I can. It'll just be a little while, that's all."

A tall, thin, dark-haired lady in a long white coat enters Pablo's room. Tino jumps off the bed and straightens up the sheet.

"Pablo, how are you doing?"

"Better today. The pain is startin' to go away. I think becoming right handed for a while is going to be the hardest thing to deal with, though."

"Good to hear you're feeling better, and we'll get you back to being left handed as soon as we can."

"You have a couple of visitors waiting to see you, so I'll come back in a bit and talk to you."

"Okay, thanks."

Tino looks at Pablo and gives a big smile. "That is one hot nurse."

"That, little bro, is my surgeon, *Doctor* Megan Batista." Pablo smiles with raised eyebrows at his grinning little brother. "I may have to stay a few extra days to be sure I'm all right."

"What a chimbo."

"Hey, I'm not faking, I just want to be sure I'm healthy enough to leave."

"Yeah, right."

Jake Bartels and another suited man walk into Pablo's room.

"Hey, Jake. What's up?" Tino greets with a smirk.

"Hi, Tino. Are you managing your brother's injury?"

"Hi, Mr. Bartels. Don't pay any attention to him," Pablo says.

Tino leaves and closes the sliding glass door to the room behind him.

Pablo pulls himself up in the bed and winced at the pain. "Please come in and sit down."

"Pablo, this is Pete Gibson, the Booter's attorney. We want to go over the contract with you today and make sure you understand it."

Pablo makes a slight adjustment to the sling that holds his left arm next to his body.

"Are you up to this, Pablo?"

"Yes, of course, Mr. Bartels."

Pablo glances out of the glass door. He sees his friend Tony and another friend, Jimmy Reed, talking with Tino.

"Pete will go over the entire contract, and then, if you have any questions, you can ask. Okay?"

Pablo glances out again, and Tony and Jimmy Reed are gone.

"Pablo, this is a standard sports contract that you can go over with your attorney and your family before signing, if you like. The team is prepared to offer you this salary." Pete Gibson points to the contract as Pablo's eyes get bigger and bigger, "and this sign-on bonus."

Jake is enjoying Pablo's response to the figures.

"And, of course, the team will pick up the hospitalization and physical therapy associated with your injury."

"So I'm on the team?"

Jake offers a handshake. "Yes, Pablo, you are on the team."

"Because of the injury?"

"No, Pablo, because of your talent. Coach Miller was ready to give the okay after he saw some of the tapes I sent him. You got this on your ability, not out of pity."

Pete offers Pablo congratulations as well and then goes back to business. "Of course, per contract, as soon as you are discharged, you will be expected to report to the academy facility every day for physical therapy and orientation during the rehab process. You will meet with coaches and other team members to discuss strategies and other team business."

Pablo shakes his head as if he didn't understand a thing Pete just said.

"So are we good?"

"Yes, we are. Where do I sign?"

"Pablo, I would suggest you go over this with your people first, and then sign. Once you've been through the contract, bring it over to the office, and we will process it."

"Well, Mr. Gibson, I don't really have any people."

"Then, I would suggest you go over it carefully with your folks. All right?"

"Of course."

Jake shakes Pablo's hand again. "Welcome aboard, Pablo. You're a Manhattan Booter. Just don't show the contract to Tino. He may want to negotiate it."

Chapter 6

Jake Bartels, Pete Gibson, Coach Miller, and Pablo Morales all stand in the middle of the team locker room. Pablo is obviously nervous as he shifts his weight from one foot to the other. His pulls up the collar of his shirt to make sure it covers the scar from his shoulder surgery. He looks over to the right and sees his name on a gold plaque on one of the open lockers.

Coach is quick to call the team to order.

"All right, fellas. Settle down. This here is Pablo Morales, our newest forward and youngest player."

"Have him stand up, Coach."

"He is sta . . . Never mind, Kirkwood. He's a bit short, but he's scrappy, and he can out maneuver most of you. Many of you saw him go down on the field a couple months ago at tryouts, but he's signed, he's back, and he's ready to work. We have our first game of the season in a few weeks. I don't know if he'll be ready or not, but we'll see how he responds to practice. Doc says he's healed up nicely and should be fine if he takes it slow for a while."

"All right, Morales, find your locker and get dressed. You know Adam Cole, he's the team captain. He can introduce you to the staff. Then come out and get warmed up."

"Okay. Thanks, Coach."

Pablo savors the moment to look at the locker with his name on it for a minute. He gets dressed and hangs his silver chain on the hook in the back.

Adam introduces Pablo to the trainers and shows him the training room, a room he was introduced to earlier under different circumstances. He sees the film room, where he is expected to invest some time, and he meets Les Anderson, the attendant for the locker room.

"Nice to meet you, Pablo. If you need anything—towels or whatever—just let me know."

"All right, thanks, Mr. Anderson."

There are a couple of suits standing around shaking hands with everybody. Pablo isn't sure what they are doing, but Adam walks by them rather quickly and says, "You can meet them later. They work up in the office."

A short while later, Adam escorts Pablo out to the field, and they both begin to warm up together. Pablo gets into it right away. He begins with some footwork, bouncing the soccer ball from one knee to the other, from one foot to the other and then passing it from his knee to Adam and back again. Coach Miller is stunned as he watches Pablo control the ball. He gets the attention of the assistant coaches, and they watch as Pablo has drawn the looks of most of the team as he and Adam continue to put on a show on the sidelines.

"But can he do that in a game?"

Coach Miller turns to see who is asking. "Kirkwood, I'm going to put this kid one-on-one with you, and if he scores on you, you're buyin' everybody dinner tonight."

"Yeah, no problem, Coach."

Chapter 7

"Thanks, Kirk. This was the best prime rib I have ever eaten. Of course, I prefer *yucca* and *papas criollas*, but this was really good."

Pablo is seated in the center of a big table with all his teammates in the main dining room of The Capital Grille in Paramus, New Jersey.

Chapter 8

Jake Bartels is seated at the big round table in the conference room in the academy facility. Pete Gibson, the Booter's lawyer, is there as well. Coach Miller and Pablo enter, and the mood grows somber. All are quiet.

Jake motions for Pablo to be seated. Pablo can't imagine what this is about, but he knows it is not for another free steak dinner.

Jake draws everyone's attention by pulling some papers out of his leather portfolio. The paper shuffling is the only sound that is heard.

Jake finally breaks the deafening silence. "Pablo, this meeting concerns two very important issues, both of which could impact you as a player, here in New Jersey and as a member of Major League Soccer. The first issue may come as a surprise, and that is that the staff here has reviewed the tape of your tryout, and there is strong evidence that Tony Drago intentionally caused your injury."

Pablo's mouth flies open, and he is obviously taken back by this information.

"It is clear to all that have looked at it, including the assistant district attorney, that there are grounds for criminal assault and other charges."

Pete Gibson chimes in, "Pablo, it appears that he came charging across the field at you, and when you jumped in the air, he purposely hit your legs in order to bring you down."

"I can't believe he would do that. He's my best friend."

Pete continues, "Given his poor performance on the field just prior to yours, and knowing that the team was prepared to only pick one of you, he certainly had motive and he had opportunity."

"The question, Pablo, is do you want to press charges against Tony?"

Without thinking, Pablo remarks, "No, of course not. He's my friend. It was just an accident. Things like that happen in sports all the time."

"Well, Pablo, accidents may happen all the time but not motivated accidents with intent to injure a fellow player, not to mention a friend that you have had since junior high."

"I just can't believe that he would do that."

Everyone in the room takes a long pause.

"You need to think about this, Pablo, and let me know if you would like to proceed with litigation."

"What's that?"

"That's legal action, Pablo."

"Coach, what should I do? I mean, I got to think about this for a while, ya know?"

Coach, not in his usual booming voice, says, "Well, Pablo, take time and think about it. We can talk about it later, and you are welcome to look at the tape if you like. But take your time to consider all of the possibilities that may come from any decision you make."

"Pablo?" Jake pulls a document out of his leather portfolio and hands it to Pablo. "Do you know what this is?"

"Yes."

Pablo drops his head to the desk. He slowly shakes his head back and forth.

He lifts his head and holds it in his hands.

His eyes begin to well with tears.

He looks down at it.

A single tear spatters as it drops on the parchment.

"It's my birth certificate."

Jake holds it up just a few inches from Pablo's face. "Yeah, well, it's a fake."

Chapter 9

Pablo is alone standing in front of his locker. He pulls his backpack out from under the leather Manhattan Booter's carry-on bag in the locker that was given to him by the equipment manager and begins to drop in his personal items.

Swagger deodorant.

Toothbrush.

Electric razor.

His silver chain with the single emerald.

"That's a nice necklace, Pablo." Pablo turns to see who has come up behind him.

"Oh, hi, Mr. Anderson."

"Going somewhere?"

"Yes, sir. Back home. I got kicked off the team. And, I have to pay all the money back. Plus, I will probably never be picked up by another MLS team once this gets out."

"Not necessarily."

"What do you mean?"

"Come back in the office with me."

"I can't go back in there."

"Sure you can. Come on."

Mr. Anderson leads Pablo back into the office.

"Excuse me, Coach Miller."

"Oh, hi, Les. We're kinda in a meeting here."

"Yes, I know, Coach. But I have something to say about this situation, and you all might just think it's important."

"Okay, Les, go ahead."

"It's a story that will clear up a lot of things with Pablo."

"With Pablo?"

"Yes, sir."

"Well, let's hear it, then."

"Andrea and I met when we were just teenagers back in Colombia. We were both eighteen. I don't think either one of us had dated before, so everything about the two of us was new to both of us. We were together all the time, and when we weren't together, we were talking on the phone to one another. Both of our last names were Santiago, so everybody just assumed we were married. She got pregnant, and we were both excited to start a family, although neither one of us had any idea what was about to happen. She was one of twelve children, so she knew a lot about raising kids. I knew nothing. I was raised by a grandmother who was drunk most of the time, and the rest of what I learned, I picked up on the street. Anyway, our son was born, and we were both very happy until the reality of and the responsibilities for raising a family set in.

"We both struggled for many years. One of Andrea's older brothers went to the States and made a life as a real estate broker. He knew many bankers, and on one of his many trips back to Bogota, he told Andrea that there was a way to get her to New York. She listened carefully but knew the reality of it was remote. He said that if she would agree to marry a friend of his, who was from New York, she could move there and raise our son. His name was Jack Morales. He wanted twelve thousand dollars. I knew this was next to impossible, but we agreed that somehow we would make this happen and get her and the child to the States to make a better life.

"Then, the next problem. She got pregnant again. I did everything I could to earn money, and we both put everything we earned away. Tino was born the following year."

Pablo leans forward in his chair. "What a minute, Tino is my brother's name, and Andrea is my mother's name."

Les holds his hand up to Pablo as if to quiet him. Pablo is stunned by this story but sits quietly. "Anyway, paying off all of the medical expenses took most of our savings. There was no end in sight until I ran into Tuco, a real Colombian thug. He was charming, with a seductive personality, and was also a big-time thief. He and I devised a plan to steal from a bank that somehow he had access to, and according to Tuco, neither we nor the money could ever be found.

"So, we did. Unfortunately, I was caught and sentenced to La Modelo prison in Bogota. While I was in prison, my cellmate, who was an American teacher, taught me English, and I, in turn, taught other inmates English. My command of English became my ticket out of prison.

"Andrea got the money through Tuco, who had escaped capture, and paid and married Jack Morales. To get Pablo registered in school, he took the name Pablo Morales. Tuco also arranged to have a second birth certificate made. That's the one in front of you, there on the table.

"I eventually traveled up through Mexico, paid a coyote to get me across the Rio Grande, and settled here in Jersey. Since I spoke exceptional English, I Americanized my name from Leonardo Santiago to Les Anderson and was readily accepted in the community."

Chapter 10

"That is an incredible story." Jake looks at Coach and at Pablo. "I mean, this is a movie waiting to be made. There's no way you can make this stuff up."

Pablo is in shock. "Mr. Anderson, you're my father."

"Yes, Pablo, I'm your father."

They both stand and stare at each other, not knowing what to do, or, for that matter, what to feel.

"Last week, when I was cleaning, I saw the silver chain with one Colombian emerald in it, hanging in your locker while you were at practice. I gave it to you back in Bogota when you were little. I knew then that you were my son. Our paths have crossed again."

Chapter 11

Pablo walks to the players' locker room when he gets inside the stadium.

"Hey, Rolo." Someone is shouting, but Pablo doesn't hear.

"Rolo!"

Pablo looks around and sees a couple of figures through the big iron fence.

"Rolo!"

Pablo recognizes the voice and walks toward them.

It is Tony and Jimmy Reed.

Pablo walks up to the fence with Tony and Jimmy Reed looking through as if they were really behind bars.

"What's up, Tony?" Now, with attitude, he says, "How's my best friend?"

"Rolo, I just wanted to come here and talk to you. I came to the hospital to visit you, but Tino said you were busy. I saw Bartels and another guy in your room, so we left."

There is a long, uncomfortable pause.

"So, Rolo, I just wanted to see if you were okay after what happened."

Pablo looks at Tony, looks over to Jimmy Reed, and then back to Tony.

"Pablo, I know you saw the tape, and you know what really happened," Tony says.

"No, I didn't actually see the tape. The coaches just told me what happened."

Another long, uncomfortable pause.

Tony allows a tear to roll down his cheek. He drops his head. Jimmy Reed nudges Tony with his elbow. Silence.

Then Tony says, "Pablo, I'm sorry I did that to you. I mean, I'm really sorry."

"Tony, that little stunt laid me up for almost eight weeks. I have a steel plate on my collarbone, and my shoulder may never be the same again."

Tony nods in agreement.

"I'm lucky I'm on the team at all."

"I mean, I couldn't blame you if you never talked to me again. But if it will help, the coaches tell me that I will probably never be eligible to play for any professional soccer team . . . ever."

"No, Tony, that doesn't help. I wouldn't wish that on you."

"You're a real friend, Rolo. Not many of my other friends would have said that."

"I know, Tony." Pablo steps closer to the iron fence.

"Look, I've had a couple months like you can't imagine. I signed a contract. I lost my contract. I got my contract back. I met my father. My father met my mother."

Tony wipes that tear away and smiles. "Rolo, this is crazy."

"Look, this is my first game since I got hurt. You want to watch?"

"For real?"

"Yeah, for real. My mom and dad are coming together. Tino will be there workin' the crowd. Mr. Bartels will be up there somewhere to see if he got his money's worth."

"C'mon. Go around to the box office and give them your name. I'll make a call."

"Rolo, you can do that?"

"Yeah." Pablo smiles. "Meet me back here after the game, and we'll catch up." He offers a fist bump to his friend Tony and to Jimmy Reed.

Pablo heads back into the locker room as the other boys run off. All of his teammates wish him well as he gets dressed for his first game as a pro. Some shake hands, some bump fists, others just mess up his long hair. Not many speak. They know what he is feeling, and their silence is a sign of support and respect. He takes special care to hang his silver chain on the hook in the back of his locker. He feels eyes in the back of his head staring at him, and he turns to see his father over by the door.

"Good luck today, Pablo. *Nos vemos despues del juego.*"

Pablo smiles, "Yes, I'll see you after the game, *gracias, Papi.*"

Chapter 12

Pablo runs off the field with confidence, as if he had been playing with this team for years.

Adam comes up behind Pablo as they happily exit the field after the game.

"Morales, we couldn't have won this game without you, ya know."

"Thanks, Adam."

"What are we going to call you, anyway . . . Pablo? Rolo? Morales?"

"Let's go with Santiago."

"Santiago, it is."

As Pablo "Rolo" Santiago leaves the team locker room, he spots a group cheering for him. There's Mami, Papi, Tino, his best friend Tony, and Jimmy Reed. He is holding his game jersey. He holds it up and turns it around.

It has a big number ten below his name—Santiago.

Chapter 13

Pablo and Tino are in the front of a big house with Andrea and Les as the movers carry furniture inside. Pablo looks at his parents, smiling and shaking their heads in disbelief.

Tino rushes into his new room, looking out the window, waving at his parents standing on the lawn. Then he holds one of his brother's jerseys up against the wall where he wants to hang it. Pablo smiles and agrees with Tino. That's where it should go.

———————

Pablo dribbles around four different opponents and scores during a game. The crowd has discovered the young star and shows their appreciation for his talent. He is surrounded by his teammates as they win another game.

———

Pablo is in front of the big, new house, sitting in his BMW 240i. Tino is in the passenger seat. Pablo helps him with his seat belt. Pablo takes off. Tino looks out the moon roof and thoroughly enjoys the opulent lifestyle, which he seems to be getting used to.

———

Pablo is hoisted onto the shoulders of Kirkwood and another big Booter after he scores a goal. He is carried off the field. The stadium is full, everyone on their feet, cheering.

———

Pablo and his family are enjoying a nice dinner at the same Capitol Grille he has been to many times with his team. The family is enjoying some much needed time alone with their celebrity son.

There are two teenage girls that approach Pablo at his table and ask for his autograph and a picture. Tino stands and positions himself between the girls and Pablo. He hands the autograph books from the girls to Pablo, then takes the picture of the girls with his brother. He thanks them and they walk away, staring at the autograph. Tino is becoming quite the public relations manager.

Chapter 14

Pablo is ready to score during a game. Adam sets him up, feeding him a high pass. Pablo jumps for a header and he is hit from below.

He's down and in pain. It's his left shoulder, again. The training staff run on to the field. Billy Hill is there and calls for the golf cart right away.

The emergency squad vehicle screams as it goes down the street, strobes flickering and lights flashing.

Dr. Batista comes into the treatment room where Pablo is sitting up in the bed. Tino is there on the bed with his arm around his brother. Andrea and Les are there as well.

Coach Miller and Jake Bartels are outside the sliding glass door looking in.

Dr. Batista puts an X-Ray on the TV monitor. With a remote she zooms in on the collar bone.

"Okay, Pablo. Here it is. The collar bone is fractured again, this time in three different places. Plus, there seems to be a little involvement in the shoulder joint as well."

She motions for the coach and Bartels to come in.

"Coach, Jake, I wanted you to hear this also."

She points to the collar bone on the TV monitor.

Andrea moves closer to the bed and takes Pablo's right hand.

"The bone is shattered, Pablo. Most likely, we will not be able to repair it this time. I'll have a couple of my colleagues look at this also, but I'm suggesting, as of now, that we replace the bone with a titanium implant. There's just nothing left to repair."

The doctor turns off the TV monitor and moves closer to her patient.

"Pablo, I would characterize this as a career ending injury."

All four Santiagos have tears streaming.

Little Tino just buries his head in Pablo's right shoulder.

Coach Miller and Jake both shake their heads.

"I'm sorry, Pablo. I feel the best option is to fix it the best we can in hopes you will have use of your shoulder again. I know this is all very shocking news. Let's get you upstairs in a room. I've ordered some pain meds that will help you sleep. We will discuss this again in the morning."

"I'm going to lose my contract, ain't I?"

Jake nods his head, "Yeah, Pablo, you are. And we are going to lose a great player."

Two attendants come in and prepare to take Pablo up to his room.

Chapter 15

The sun shines in through the glass panels of the Solarium. Tino has Pablo in a wheelchair spinning him around the room.

"Tino, stop."

Tino stops spinning the chair and looks at his brother.

"Megan says you need to get more exercise."

"That's Dr. Batista, and I'm pretty sure she meant me, not you."

"Hey, I'm trying to get you back in shape."

"How about parking me over there in the shade for a little while."

Tino pushes the wheelchair around a couple of times and nearly runs into a man walking into the solarium.

Pablo recognizes the man right away.

"Coach Hutson?"

"Rolo. How you doing?"

Tino parks and locks the wheelchair. Coach Hutson pulls up a chair.

"I'm surprised to see you," Pablo says.

"Can I sit?"

"Of course, Coach. You here to see me?"

"Yes, and to talk about life after MLS."

Pablo lowers his head and mumbles. "There isn't any. How did you find out?"

"Pablo, I stay in touch with Jake Bartels. And, I had a visitor the other day."

"Who's that, Coach?"

"Drago."

"Tony?"

"The one and only."

"What did he want?"

"Well, he gave me the rundown on your injury and your surgery. He says you're feeling sorry for yourself and he wanted me to come over here and shake you up a little bit."

"Yeah, I'm down a little, but I think I'll be okay. I just have to find something to do now."

Coach gives Pablo a big smile.

"Funny you should mention that."

"Why?"

"How long 'til you get out of here?"

"Dr. Batista says about another week, then rehab for a while."

"I may have a solution for life after MLS."

Pablo looks up with a smile. "Like what?"

"Francis Lewis is starting varsity girl's soccer this year."

"That's good Coach. But I can't play on a girl's team."

"I know that. You could coach, though."

"What?"

"You heard right, Pablo."

"Coach soccer? Girl's soccer?"

"I haven't hired a coach yet."

"Why me, Coach?"

"Why not, you?"

"Well, I . . . ah . . . I don't know. I never thought of it. It was really nice of you to think of me."

"I didn't think of you. Tony Drago did. And, I concur, it's a great idea. He has even consented to assist you, if you want him."

"That would be cool, Coach."

"It's settled then?"

"Sure, I'll try it out for a while."

"I'll go back to the school and talk to the principal."

"Thanks for giving me a chance, Coach."

"This is going to work out just great, Rolo."

"Tino, let's walk Coach out."

Tino closes a big book he is reading. He hands it to Pablo as he unlocks the wheels of the chair.

Coach Hutson sees it. "What a ya readin, kid?"

"It's a textbook on sports management."

"I should have guessed."

Tino starts pushing Pablo down the hall as Coach Hutson walks beside them.

"See, Coach, or Coaches, as it were, the way I figure it, I can schedule practices for the boys and the girls on the field at different times so they don't interfere with each other or school. Then, I can be with Rolo for his practices to help him with any logistical problems. Of course, I can call Jake anytime for help. He said I could contact him if I needed to. I have his cell phone number, ya know. And, if I see any problems, Coach Miller said I could give him a call also . . ."

THE TALE OF SONNY BARLOW

T he year was 1873. The place was the Texas Tavern Saloon in Lynchburg, Virginia. Actually it was the alley in the back of the saloon. The piano could be heard through the screen door. Cigar smoke wafted out the same door.

Bobby Medina cupped his hands around his eyes and peered through the grimy screen. He took a good look inside and then directed his attention to the two large metal cans next to the brick building.

He picked through the most recent deposit in hopes of finding a fresh drop of uneaten steak bones and some leftover bread.

There were two rats who were also in competition for the steak bone lying right on top. As Bobby reached for the bone, the rats squealed and disappeared into the night.

The rat's exit frightened Bobby and he fell against one of the metal cans, which drove it into the red brick wall with a clang.

Sonny Barlow heard the clang as he passed by the alley. He rushed over and saw Bobby lying in the dirt.

Bobby saw Sonny approach. He got up and brushed himself off.

"Look, mister. I wasn't doin' nothin'. Just tryin' to get me some food.

"Hey, kid, I ain't the law. I just wanted to see if you were alright, that's all."

"Yeah, of course I'm alright. I just slipped."

Bang. Bang.

Two shots rang out and both Sonny and Bobby stood perfectly still.

Chaos and commotion were heard from inside the saloon. Sonny approached the screen door.

The screen door burst open. A huge man of at least 300 pounds backed in the doorway, holding his chest.

The white apron he was wearing was stained with blood.

The big man wobbled a bit and then fell like a giant oak.

Bobby backed out of the way, "I'm gettin' the hell outta here."

"No, you're not," Sonny told him. "You know where the doc's office is?"

"Yeah, I think."

"Okay, you run as fast as you can over there and bring the doc here."

Sonny heard the street filling with people, but nobody came around the back door.

Sonny went right to work.

He heard the sucking of the wound on the right side of the man's chest and quickly grabbed one of the bar towels from the big man's apron strings. He put pressure on the hole in his chest as he looked for other wounds.

He pulled the man's shirt free and saw another bullet wound in the right side below the ribs. He held pressure on the chest wound.

With his free hand, he attempted to roll the rotund man up on his left side. He took one of the trash cans and wedged it between the brick wall and the barkeep.

Bobby appeared with Doc Stanton, who, in his seventies was barely able to stand himself. He looked at what Sonny had done.

"What happened here?"

"Two gunshots, Doc. One in the belly, looks like it went right through and this chest wound. I got it plugged with a bar towel for now."

By now, there were several people that had gathered to see what happened.

"You've done everything right so far, but we have to get him over to my office real quick. You did right by gettin' that good lung up."

Sonny looked around at a few of the town folks.

"Hey, can a couple of you fellas get that buckboard backed up over here?"

The towns people started following the orders. There was commotion, but it was not a scene of chaos.

"We're goin' to need about six of you fellas to lift this guy."

A handful of townspeople gently lifted the big man into the buckboard. Sonny instructed one of the men to hold pressure on the chest wound. The driver took off nice and slow. The old doc and Bobby followed the wagon as it crossed the street.

The old doc put his hand on Bobby's shoulder.

"Where is that young man?"

Bobby stopped in the middle of the street and looked all around. He and the old doc both looked in all directions.

Bobby shrugged his shoulders, "He's gone."

———

Kaboom! A shotgun blast ripped through a tree line directly in front of eighteen-year-old Sonny Barlow as he rode along a riverbed. He was on the outskirts of Silver City, New Mexico. Sonny was a young man traveling through the Old West.

"Hey! Hold your fire!" Sonny quickly slid out of the saddle on his old mare and headed for the nearest tree for some cover. "Hold your fire! Don't shoot! I don't mean any harm."

"Who's out there?" yelled the shooter.

"Name's Sonny Barlow. Just passin' through," he yelled, now responding from behind the security of a big tree.

"Git out here where I can see ya."

"Okay, okay, just don't shoot." Sonny held his hands high in the air and walked out from behind the tree slowly toward the mystery voice. As he stepped into a small clearing, he could see the shooter. "You the one doing the shootin'?"

"Yeah. I thought you was a turkey. Good thing for you I don't know how to use this thing so good."

The shooter motioned for Sonny to join him in a makeshift camp. Sonny tied his mare up to a tree branch and headed for the campsite.

The shooter never took his eyes off of Sonny.

"You say your name was Sonny?"

"Yeah, Sonny Barlow."

"Is that your real name?"

"Nope. My real name's John Thomas Barlow the second, but my Pa always called me Sonny. What's yours?"

"Henry McCarty."

Sonny asked, "What do people call you?"

"Henry McCarty."

Sonny rolled his eyes.

"Do you want to sit?" asked Henry.

"Sure." Sonny thought Henry looked very young.

"You from around these parts?" asked Henry.

"No, I'm from back East. Virginia way. I sorta ran away from my father and his medical practice and I just happened to end up here. I'm headed for the mountains in Nevada territory where all the silver is, and thought I might do some silver mining . . . You gonna offer me some coffee?"

"I ain't got no coffee."

"Well, I do." Sonny headed for his saddlebags. Henry reached for his shotgun again. When Sonny heard the hammer cock, he pulled the saddlebags slowly away from the back of his saddle. He rummaged for an old pot and headed back to where his new-found friend, Henry McCarty, sat.

"I can make pretty good coffee. If you could get a fire started, it would help." Sonny looked around for Henry's belongings, but he didn't see anything. He didn't want to get too nosey because Henry still had the shotgun close by. Henry watched Sonny intently as he made the coffee.

"You're kinda young to be travelin' around all alone, ain't ya?" asked Henry.

"Me? You don't even look like you shave yet. How old are you?"

Henry proudly responded, "I was fourteen last November."

Sonny stared at Henry for a moment. "I remember fourteen. I used to drive my father's buggy. He's a medical doctor back in Virginia. I'd drive so he could sleep between the house calls he made out in the country. My Ma died when I was born, so he raised me . . . sorta."

"What do you mean, sorta?" asked Henry.

Sonny took a long pause and then continued. "I've always had trouble reading, but he never had the time to help me. In fact, I can barely read at all. So I got tired of the way things were and decided to change them. I left and never turned back. I took some of those medical books of his that I used to carry around for him all the time and headed west."

"What good are the books gonna do for ya?"

"Well, I wasn't sure, at first. Maybe I just wanted to steal them from my Pa to make him angry. But those books have helped."

Sonny remembered back to the time a few months ago when he first realized their value. "I had just left Virginia and I had been talking to a little boy in an alley behind a saloon. The kid was scrounging for food. He couldn't have been more than six years old. He had told me he was running away from home. All of a sudden, the back door flew open and the bartender fell out.

"He had blood all over his white apron. I guess he got shot in a brawl or something and was tryin' to escape when he fell. I grabbed the towel from his apron strings and tried to patch him up as fast as I could, just like I'd seen in those books.

"I sent the kid to get the doctor. The old town doc showed up and was impressed at how I had handled everything.

"I thought, hey, why not use the books all the way to Nevada? Hell, I can pull teeth, cure colic in a horse, deliver a calf, splint broken bones and the like. I go by the pictures in the medical books, plus I learned a lot by watching my Pa all those years."

"Sure sounds like your pa was a good man. You're too hard on him, Sonny. You should give him another try."

"Na. Had to go."

"At least you've got a pa. Anything's better than no parents at all."

"You an orphan?" asked Sonny.

Henry sat back and stared at the horizon. "You ever hear of galloping consumption?"

Sonny didn't even have to think about his answer. He had seen it so many times. "That's the common name for tuberculosis with pneumonia. Why?"

Henry responded matter-of-factly. "My Ma's got it. I think she's going to die soon."

"There's a good chance, Henry. Is she getting any treatment?"

"I don't know. I left right after she got married again to her new husband. He's a lot younger than she is."

Henry picked up a stick and started drawing circles in the loose dirt. "So where are you headed?"

Sonny continued. "Well, like I said, I'm headed up in the mountains to try my hand at silver mining. How hard can it be? I thought I would travel through Texas to the Rio Grande and follow it North. I ended up here."

Henry shook his head. "Well, you're a long way from the Rio

Grande. Plus, you already crossed it. You got trouble readin' maps, too?"

Sonny grimaced and reached for the hot pot. "Coffee's done."

———————————

The next several months were lonely and arduous as Sonny made his way alone toward Nevada, not via the Rio Grande. Henry had helped him out with directions; he might have ended up in Colorado without them.

On the way, Sonny carried through on his plans. He delivered a baby in Ash Fork, Arizona, patched up a few ranchers here and there, got a few day's work framing a building, and did odd jobs to get his keep.

He had been headed up the mountains for several weeks and he knew he was getting close to where he wanted to do his silver mining.

———————————

Bang! The two doors of the Napias City School flew open and the students of the seventh and eighth grades exploded out of the building as if they were shot from a cannon. They pushed and shoved down the rickety wooden steps. Sara tripped and fell and landed on the bottom step. Jeb tripped over her and nearly landed right on top of Sara.

Jeb got right in her face. "How did I ever get you for a partner anyway?"

Sara paid no attention; she was so intent on her mission. She got up, brushed off her dress, and the two of them took off together across the schoolyard. In seconds, they were away from the others and into the open fields. From there they quickly headed north.

Jeb had a grin on his face. "This is one of the best ideas our teacher's ever come up with," he said.

Sara took big steps to try to keep up with Jeb. "This will be a chance to learn a lot."

Jeb fired back his response without even looking at Sara. "Who cares about learnin' anything? This is a day outside, no teacher, no books, and no rules. Hurry up, will ya?"

Sara finally grabbed Jeb by the shirtsleeve to slow him down a bit. They continued to walk. "Remember, this is going to be a graded assignment and if your tomfoolery gets me into trouble, I'll report you to Mrs. Donovan."

Jeb fired back again, "Yeah, sure! Just because you're the teacher's pet don't mean that I am too."

"Doesn't!"

Jeb stared at her. "What?"

"*Doesn't* mean that I am too."

Jeb wore a disgusted look on his face as the pair continued on.

Jeb and Sara, completely by themselves now, walked along the roadside. Sara looked back and saw the town disappear in the distance. They strolled for a couple of miles.

"Jeb, I want to do a really good job. If I can show Mrs. Donovan how well I'm doing, maybe she can help me become a teacher someday."

Jeb had an unusually serious look on his face. It seemed to Sara that he had softened a bit. "This really does mean a lot to you, doesn't it, Sara?"

"Of course it does." She stopped and looked up into a big tree that was fifty yards in front of them. Her eyes seemed to grow bigger and bigger. Her heart leaped. "And I think I see just the thing to make this great!"

Jeb didn't seem to see anything, or at least he didn't see what Sara had spotted.

"What do you see?

"See that big oak tree over there?" she asked.

"Where?"

"The one hanging over the cliff?"

He finally spotted it. "Yeah."

Sara motioned to Jeb. "Let's get closer."

They approached the oak and discovered what appeared to be an eagle's nest. It certainly was large enough, nestled in the base of three sturdy branches.

Jeb was still clueless. "So what? What's the project?"

Sara was happy to explain it to him, wondering when he would get it. "Well, let's see if there's anything in it."

"What do you mean, *let's see*?"

"Well, *you*, actually. I can't climb up there; I might rip my dress, and if I rip my dress . . . "

"Okay, okay, I'll do it," he said.

Sara watched as Jeb began the long climb up the huge tree. He tried to make it look easy, as if he were preserving his image as the masculine example of the species. She smiled. He struggled for a while, then she saw him get a foothold as he reached a big branch.

He paused, then continued to climb. Sara stood on her toes when he was just about able to look inside the nest. He stretched another foot or so, but couldn't see anything so he pulled up on another branch and then looked inside. Sara waited to hear what he'd found.

"It's a bust," he yelled down. "No eagles. No eggs. The nest is empty."

All that work, she thought.

Suddenly she heard a loud crack.

"Jeb, you'd best come down. I don't think that tree is safe."

There was a longer, softer cracking sound. Jeb's face looked panicked. "You might be right."

Jeb had no sooner said that than there was a final long, cracking sound. The limb on which Jeb was lying broke off cleanly from the huge tree. Jeb hollered as he and the limb disappeared off the edge of the cliff.

A few seconds went by.

There was a crash.

Sara raced to the edge of the cliff.

There was silence.

She wanted to look but didn't want to see what she knew had happened.

She slowly peered over the edge.

She looked down.

"Jeb? Jeb? I *told* you to come down from there." He was lying on a small ridge about eight to ten feet below, but some hundred feet above the canyon floor.

She saw his chest moving very slowly. He looked alive. She looked quickly for any other signs of life. She knew she couldn't get down and she knew she couldn't get him up. Sara didn't know what to do.

Jeb needed help, so she got up to run for help. She ran to the road and through streaming tears was able to see the distant figure of a man on horseback.

"*Help*! . . . *Help*! I need help!" she shouted.

The man apparently heard her because he stopped the horse.

Sonny Barlow turned his horse around and headed to the source of the girl's cries.

"Help! Help! Hurry!"

Sonny reached the scene where Jeb had fallen. He got off his mare and handed the reins to Sara.

"Here . . . hold her." Sonny stood and looked over the edge. He estimated the ridge where Jeb lay measured only about four by eight feet, maybe a little bigger. With the exception of his breathing, Jeb lay lifeless, with the large broken tree limb beside him. Sonny saw that some blood dripped from the back of Jeb's head onto the tree limb.

Sara watched Sonny, but he gave her no indication he would be able to help. He saw her from the corner of his eye. She looked up at him, as he stood with the sun backlighting his golden hair as if he were her guardian angel.

Sonny turned his attention to Sara and sighed deeply. He saw a frantic, scared thirteen-year-old who looked to him for help. He looked back down at Jeb. Seconds became minutes.

She asked, "Maybe you could drop a rope and pull Jeb up."

Sonny held up a hand for silence. He needed to think. Finally, he spoke. "Great idea, but I don't have a rope."

Sara began to cry.

"What are you kids doing out here?"

She pointed to the tree. "Looking for eagle eggs."

Sonny looked up and sighed. He was trying to help. He knew that her eyes never left him as he slowly and methodically assessed the situation.

He continued to look over the edge. Finally, without warning, Sonny disappeared over the cliff, giving the girl no indication whether he had fallen or had jumped. He saw her peer over the edge. Sonny checked Jeb over like the town doc would examine a patient.

"Is he going to be okay?"

"Well, he ain't dead." Sonny continued to assess Jeb's condition, then he looked up at the edge of the cliff to Sara.

"Okay, kid. Listen to me very carefully. Your friend here, Jeb? He's hurt real bad. We need help and you're going to have to go get it. How far away is the nearest town?"

"Treasure Hill, just a few miles south of here."

"Are you a good rider?"

"Yes sir. Real good."

"You got a doctor in that town?"

"Yes sir."

"Okay. Go get help. Take my mare and throw the saddlebags down here."

"Yes, sir."

She dropped the heavy saddlebags down to Sonny, climbed on the mare, and looked down again over the cliff. "Hey, what's your name?"

"Sonny. Sonny Barlow. Now git going."

Sara rode off and Sonny returned with his saddlebags to Jeb. He had moved Jeb onto his back. He unpacked some bandages. There was a large wound on Jeb's head. Sonny wrapped Jeb's head in a bandage as best he could. He pulled a big book out of his saddlebag and began to turn through the pages. He looked at Jeb and although he was still unconscious, his breathing was regular.

He pulled a pocket watch out of his pant's pocket. He opened it; he checked Jeb's pulse. On the cover of the pocket watch, there was a picture of a man in a suit. After he checked Jeb's pulse, Sonny stared at the picture for a minute.

"I almost wish you were here to help me with this one, instead of off helping someone else, like usual." Sonny thought back to what Henry had said to him all those months ago: "Sounds like your pa was a good guy."

He shook his head and focused again on Jeb. "It's just this kid and me now. I hope he's got a strong will to live, cause he's going to need it." He closed the watch cover and replaced it in his pocket.

Sonny cradled Jeb's badly injured head in his hands. Jeb's breathing continued to be slow. Sonny gently raised Jeb's eyelids and saw two big, bright green eyes that could see absolutely nothing. As Sonny closed Jeb's eyelids, he looked up into the sky with a look of helplessness.

"You stupid kid. Did it ever occur to you and your girlfriend that there were no birds in that nest because the tree's been dead for years? The eagles were smarter than you were."

Sonny picked up the heavy textbook again and turned the pages. He continued for a minute until he came to a page with a few pictures. He studied it for a moment, closed it, and laid it down next to the broken tree limb.

Jeb began to move his legs a bit. At first, Sonny was startled, but then he watched cautiously and wondered what might happen next. The movement stopped. Other than the slow rise and fall of Jeb's chest, his body returned to a lifeless state.

"C'mon, Jeb. Hold on. Help's on the way . . . I hope."

Mrs. Donovan, the teacher of the big one-room school, was seated at a table in the rear of the classroom. There were papers and ledgers spread all over it. She was using the quiet time to catch up on her reading of the local newspaper. The *White Pine News* was Treasure Hill's only newspaper, but it was one of the best in Nevada.

Moses, the school's handyman, had just come back. He had spent his lunch hour at the Sheriff's office, talking with his friends, the town deputies, as they posted up the newest wanted posters. He entered the room to complete his daily chores. Mrs. Donovan smiled at him, stretched, and stood up.

The day had grown warm, so she turned and opened the doors to get some air inside.

She saw Sara in the distance. The girl was riding quickly—too quickly—toward town. Moses stopped dead in his tracks as he heard the girl yell for the teacher.

Sara reigned in the horse and almost fell off. She jumped down, ran up the steps of the school and into the comforting embrace of her teacher.

She sobbed in Mrs. Donovan's arms. "We need a doctor!"

"Sara, what on earth is wrong?"

"It's Jeb . . . he had an accident."

Mrs. Donovan pulled Sara from her embrace. She held her firmly by the shoulders and with a stern look in her eyes said, "Where is he now, child? Where is he?"

Sara tried to speak and cry at the same time. She gulped. "We were working on our assignment. Jeb climbed a tree to get a nest and the limb broke. He fell down on a ridge and got knocked out."

Moses headed for the back door. "I'll get him back here. I'll go hitch up the wagon." He exited the classroom as Sara continued.

"An older boy, Sonny, came along. He's with Jeb now."

Sara returned to the comforting embrace of her teacher. "Oh, Mrs. Donovan, I'm so scared. Sonny says Jeb is hurt real bad, and we didn't do our assignment, and . . ."

"Never mind about the assignment. Let's just concentrate on getting Jeb back here safely. Alright, go out back and help Moses hitch the team. You'll have to show him the way."

Sara composed herself. "I know exactly where it is. Just north of town a couple of miles. Just off the road. I even know a shortcut."

"Okay, then, you get started. I'll go for a doctor."

Sara responded with confidence. "Yes, ma'am."

Sara took off out the back door. She felt better now that she had gotten help, and she didn't even get in trouble. Sara rode Sonny's mare as Moses followed in the wagon. They didn't race in an all-out gallop, but they trotted at a good pace and finally arrived at the cliff.

They quickly dismounted and headed to the edge. Sonny, thumbing through his big book again, heard the commotion, jammed the book under a limb, stood up, and waited to see who had arrived. Sara looked over the edge in anticipation.

"How's Jeb?"

Sonny avoided answering. He spotted Moses. "You'd better come down here, ah . . . mister"

"Just call me Moses." Moses stood there and stared at Sonny for a few seconds, as if he recognized him. "Do I know you?"

"Don't think so," said Sonny.

Moses scrutinized him as if he didn't believe him. "How's the boy?"

"Not so good, Moses."

Moses grabbed a rope from the back of the wagon and tied one end to the trunk of the tree. He lowered it down to Sonny, and then he lowered himself down onto the ridge.

His face showed amazement as he saw Jeb's left leg splinted with a couple of small tree limbs and old bandages, and Jeb's head wrapped up.

"Looks like you know some about doctoring." Sonny watched Moses' gaze wander to the medical textbook laying under one of the limbs.

"You studyin' to be a doctor?"

Sonny avoided eye contact. "Somethin' like that. We need to be real careful not to move his head."

Moses did exactly what Sonny said to do. They began to move Jeb slowly. All four hands worked together. When they rolled Jeb up on his side to get a blanket under him, he winced a bit.

Sonny winked at Moses, "That's a good sign."

Moses looked directly at Sonny, "What all is wrong with the boy?"

"Well, for starters, he's got a bad head wound and a concussion. His left leg is busted in a couple of places and he's in shock."

"Can we get him out of here by ourselves?"

Sonny responded, "Yeah, sure. If you want to kill him. We're going to need more help."

"Well, the teacher went to get a doctor. Our hospital in Treasure Hill's got a half a dozen. One will be coming soon."

A small buggy drew closer. Sara yelled and waved her arms to get its attention. Mrs. Donovan and a doctor pulled up close to the edge of the cliff and jumped out. Mrs. Donovan embraced Sara, acknowledged Moses, and then looked over the edge of the cliff.

She saw Jeb for the first time since earlier that day. Her eyes teared up, but immediately she regained her composure. She looked down at Sonny.

"How's Jeb?"

Sonny didn't even look her way. "About the same."

"Are you Sonny?"

Sonny responded to the sound of her soft voice. He looked up at her. "Yes, ma'am. Sonny Barlow."

"Well, Sonny Barlow, it looks like you have things under control for now."

Dr. Peter Jensen got his bag out of the buggy and headed for the edge of the cliff. "What happened here, son?"

"Well, this kid was up in that tree, and the branch broke off. I was ridin' along, and I heard Sara yellin for help . . . so, I helped." Sonny was curious about the doctor. "You from the hospital?"

"Yes, I'm Dr. Jensen, chief of staff. Looks like you patched him up pretty well. Why don't we take a closer look at him?"

There wasn't much room on the ridge, so Moses climbed back up as Dr. Jensen lowered himself down.

"I did the best I could."

Dr. Jensen did a quick evaluation of Jeb and Sonny's work and looked toward the top of the cliff.

"Okay, we're going to need everybody's help to raise this boy off this ridge."

Not much time passed before Jeb was lying in the back of the wagon on a blanket. Dr. Jensen and Sonny climbed in the back to stay with him as Moses jumped to the front and turned to watch them make Jeb as comfortable as they could.

Dr. Jensen motioned to Moses.

"Okay, Moses, real easy now."

Mrs. Donovan took the doctor's buggy and Sara jumped up to ride Sonny's mare. They pulled away slowly for the ride into town. Sara knew there was hope for Jeb. She followed behind the wagon.

As the procession slowly moved away from the sight, Sara forced herself to turn and look back at the scene. The rope was still attached to the trunk of the big tree.

She worried. A hundred *what ifs* went through her mind. *What if the ride to town is too much? What if he's really, really hurt?* She gulped. *What if he dies?*

Sonny was strategically placed at Jeb's head. Dr. Jensen was by his side. Sonny held the injured head gently.

"How's this, Doctor?"

"You've got to hold it like that all the way to town, Sonny."

"I can do it, sir."

The wagon rolled at a steady, gentle pace. Moses turned and looked in the back often, as if he wanted to make sure his driving was smooth enough. Sara, riding Sonny's mare, never took her eyes from Jeb.

Dr. Jensen observed Sonny Barlow.

"You've got real gentle hands, Sonny. That's a gift."

"Well, that's the only gift he ever gave me."

"Who gave you, son?"

"My father. The great Dr. Barlow. I was named after him. I'm John Thomas Barlow the second."

"Your father?"

Sonny nodded. "Living with Pa wasn't so great. My ma died when I was born. My father wasn't around. He was off deliverin' someone else's baby. Didn't have any brothers or sisters. He and Ma didn't even have time for that. He was too busy, and he never got me any proper schoolin'."

"A doctor's life is demanding sometimes. It gets in the way of family."

Sonny thought about that. Henry had suggested that perhaps he had been too hard on his pa. "One thing about him I had to respect was that he loved his work. Nothin' came above his work, not even me. I learned a lot watchin' and helpin' whenever I could. I delivered a baby when I was just fifteen. That was one of the biggest thrills of my life."

Dr. Jensen smiled. Sonny knew by the doctor's expression that he had experienced that same feeling. He wondered how many babies Dr. Jensen had delivered.

"You thinking about going to medical college and becoming a doctor like your father?"

Sonny shook his head. "I don't really want to be anything like my pa." While talking to Dr, Jensen, Sonny never took his eyes off of Jeb. "About six months ago I left him. I took this bag of medicine and those books there in my saddlebags and headed out here. Just been driftin' ever since, helping folks along the way, when I can. I use that book of treatments sometimes."

Dr. Jensen picked up the book. There was a page marked with a small ribbon. The doctor turned to the page and discovered a few drawings of head injuries. "Is this the book you used to treat Jeb?"

"Yes, sir, that's the one."

"You read all about it?"

He looked up at Dr. Jensen. "Uh . . . yeah."

Dr. Jensen changed the subject. "You know, Sonny, we've got a booming mining town here. And a very progressive hospital with several doctors and nurses from all over the country. With some proper training, you could really help us out.

You seem to have a real calm way about you. We see a lot of injuries from the mines and a person with cool reasoning like yourself could have a great future."

Sonny stared down at his patient. He felt his skin burn. He was sure the doctor noticed his face turn red. "I like workin' alone, Dr. Jensen. It's been like that all my life." Before the doctor could say anything else, Sonny quickly changed the subject.

"How much further, Moses?"

━━━━━━━━━━

Mrs. Donovan, Sara, and Sonny sat quietly on some wooden benches at the end of a long empty hallway in the Treasure Hill Hospital. Hours had passed since they had brought Jeb in. It was now dark outside and streaks of moonlight were shining in the few small windows from the outside. Dr. Jensen stepped out of a treatment room down the hall.

He was dressed in a long white coat, looking very doctorly. Several nurses scurried in and out of rooms. The three of them watched and waited; there was nothing else they could do. Dr. Jensen walked slowly toward the trio with a somber look on his face and his head down. He had taken this same walk before. It was a difficult walk to make, but not half as difficult as the news he now had to share.

Sara knew.

She began to cry.

She buried her face in Mrs. Donovan's arms.

The teacher knew, too.

Tears began to flow easily. She broke out a kerchief to wipe them away.

Sonny sat motionless.

He had a blank stare on his face.

He appeared to be frozen in time.

His eyes were dry, though.

Dr. Jensen sat on a bench across the hall from the others.

He was in great pain, but he knew he must remain professional.

He lifted his head slowly and spoke. "It's hard enough when they're old, but when they're just thirteen . . ." He took a long pause to gather energy for the final blow. "We did everything we could do, but Jeb died."

Dr. Jensen took another long pause as he looked from Sonny to Sara to the teacher. Sonny remained still. Sara's faced was buried in the teacher's arms. Mrs. Donovan lost her composure and sobbed openly. When she quieted, the doctor asked her, "Have his folks been notified?"

Mrs. Donovan took a moment and then said, "Well, actually, he's an orphan, Dr. Jensen. Both his folks were killed in an explosion near the mine several months ago. He lived at the school, in the back store room."

She reflected for a moment. "He was the best kid, you know. He hated school, but he could out-work every other student in his class."

Mrs. Donovan stood up, and pulled Sara with her. They started to leave. They walked about ten feet, and the teacher turned slowly and looked at Sonny Barlow, still frozen in time on the bench.

"Thank you for all you did, Sonny."

He didn't look up, but he responded in a sorrowful tone of voice, "It wasn't enough."

Mrs. Donovan nodded. She turned away; she and Sara left the

hospital. Dr. Jensen moved to the bench where Sonny was seated and sat beside him. There was a long, uncomfortable pause.

"You know, Sonny, if you gave a hundred percent, then there is nothing to apologize for. Jeb had an extensive head injury and was in deep shock. I doubt that anyone here could have saved him."

The doctor saw Sonny's face change from a blank stare to an expression of confusion. Then a look of torment. *Sonny must be wrestling with his past,* the doctor thought.

"I could have helped him more, I know," said Sonny. "I had the medicine and the books. The books ... the books ... if only I could ..."

"Could what, Sonny?"

"If only I could read. I can't read, Dr. Jensen."

A shocked Dr. Jensen now recalled how Jeb's head and left leg were bandaged precisely the way they were demonstrated in the textbook. "So how is it that you use the books for treating people?"

"I go by the pictures, sir, and what my pa taught me when I traveled with him. A pretty stupid way to practice medicine, huh?"

"Yes, Sonny. Very stupid."

Sonny's eyes darted to the side. "How many people have I harmed by looking at pictures instead of reading words?

"Sonny, I think a better question would be how many people can you help in the future by going about it the right way?"

"The right way?"

"Yes. Learn how to read, then continue your education in a medical college and practice medicine the way it was intended."

Sonny shook his head in embarrassment. "I couldn't start now."

"This is precisely the time to start. You've already jumped the greatest hurdle, admitting that you can't read. Now, focus on getting the job done."

The two of them sat there together for a few minutes, their backs to the wall, both staring out at the floor.

Sonny suddenly said, "I'd do it for Jeb."

"You should do it for Sonny. And for all the patients that will need your expertise someday. We need good doctors, Sonny, and you could be a good one."

Sonny actually mustered a bit of a smile. "Maybe if I could read, I could actually write to my father and tell him. I'd love to see the look on his face when he receives a letter that I actually wrote. I wonder if he even knows I can't read."

Sonny shivered when he thought of Jeb dying as an orphan, a boy who would never be missed by his father. Henry's words now haunted him. They floated through his mind, *"Anything's better than having no parent at all."*

Sonny and Dr. Jensen got up from the bench and slowly continued their talk as they walked down the long hallway of Treasure Hill Hospital.

Sonny sat toward the rear of the full classroom. Mrs. Donovan had strategically placed him there so he felt a little more comfortable, sitting next to some of the bigger boys, but he was still four or five years their senior. He had been in school for months now, and since Jeb's death, he had stayed in the same back room that Jeb had lived in after his parents were killed.

Sonny would report to the hospital at first light and work there until school started at 7:30. He always stayed an hour extra at the end of the school day to study new words, grammar, and spelling with Sara. She had been a tremendous help to Sonny and she never said a word regarding his progress to any of the other students, which is what he liked best of all.

He went back to the hospital after he finished his schoolwork to complete his daily work there. Dr. Jensen had arranged a small stipend and meals at the hospital, not to mention a lot of valuable experience that he would be able to use someday in his practice.

Things appeared to be going well for Sonny. He could almost see a light at the end of the tunnel. He still couldn't bring himself to go out to the cemetery to visit Jeb's grave, though. Most of the students had been out several times; some had even planted flowers. The school had ordered a nice headstone, which had not yet arrived from California.

One afternoon after the class was excused for the day, Sara and Sonny took their usual places at the big table in the back. Moses hovered in the background, close by, as he had since Sonny had arrived.

"Sonny, you're doing very well. I don't know how much longer you're going to need my help."

Sonny noticed Sara couldn't sit still. She was obviously uncomfortable.

"Actually, you're doing so well that . . . oh, what's the use?"

"Sara, just say it out."

"I can't help you anymore after school."

Sonny was shocked. Things had been going so well.

"Why not?"

"We . . . uh, I mean, my family isn't doing so well at the mine. My Pa says the veins are drying up and there isn't as much silver as there was a few years ago."

"So how will that affect my school work?"

"I've taken work over at Miss Freeman's Boarding House sewing for her and helping with the evening meals. She pays real well, and our family really needs the money."

Sonny was relieved. "Is that all? Don't worry about not being able to work with me. Mrs. Donovan already said that she would help me anytime I needed it."

Sara exhaled, obviously relieved.

Sonny understood the circumstances. He was glad that it was nothing he had done to prompt her leaving. Sonny actually looked forward to having Mrs. Donovan tutor him after class. She was much stricter than Sara; he looked forward to the challenge.

Shortly thereafter, Mrs. Donovan took over his tutoring. The first weeks went by uneventfully. Sonny was doing well, and Mrs.

Donovan piled on the work. Sonny appreciated the one-on-one attention, and he was learning rapidly. He practiced writing every day. Mrs. Donovan told him he had nice penmanship.

One day, however, he was reading very intently and didn't notice Moses passing through the schoolroom. As he read, he could feel Moses staring at him. Moses had just returned from spending time with his deputy friends, and as usual, he had studied the wanted posters as they were placed on the wall. Moses had seen someone familiar on the wall that day.

Just as Sonny and Mrs. Donovan were about to finish for the day, they heard footsteps on the steps of the school building. Sheriff Kelly and one of his deputies entered and stood over Sonny.

Sheriff Kelly directed a question to Mrs. Donovan. "Is this kid Sonny Barlow?"

Moses left quickly through the back door.

Mrs. Donovan stood up. Sonny's jaw dropped.

Again, he asked, "Is *this* Sonny Barlow?"

Sonny and Mrs. Donovan both nodded.

"Ah, yeah. I'm Sonny Barlow. What's this about, Sheriff?"

"Do you know this person here?" The sheriff unrolled a wanted poster. It was clearly a picture of Sonny Barlow. And to Sonny's amazement, under his picture were the words: *Wanted for Murder.*

Sonny responded meekly, "Me?"

"Yeah, it's you. You're going to have to come with us until we get this sorted out."

Mrs. Donovan fired back, "There's nothing to sort out. You certainly have the wrong person. This boy is no murderer."

"What are you to this boy, ma'am?"

"I'm his teacher. He's been here for months studying and working at the hospital. He's no murderer."

"Well, ma'am, I've got a telegram on my desk that says he was involved in a murder in Lynchburg, Virginia, some time ago. Seems he shot a bartender there and then skipped town."

The teacher fired back again, "Well, your telegram is wrong."

"I have to take him in for questioning, no matter what you say. And he'll have to go back east to stand trial. Right now, I've got to take him in to custody. C'mon, son."

Sheriff Kelly and his deputy helped Sonny out of his chair and escorted him out of the school.

Sonny explained, "I didn't shoot him. I helped patch him up after he was shot. You can ask the town doc."

"Funny thing. The town doc is missing. But they had a witness. You'll have time to tell your side. All the way back to Virginia. Right now, though, you're coming with us."

———————————

Early one morning a few days later, Sonny knelt beside the small grave. It was peaceful in the cemetery. He smelled the sweet flowers that were planted around the grave. Sheriff Kelly and the deputy stood just a few feet away. They had agreed to allow Sonny a few minutes at the gravesite before heading east for his murder trial.

There was still no gravestone yet, but the morning sun had cast a defining shadow on the ground from the wooden cross that temporarily identified the grave. Sonny thought it was the nicest grave in the whole place. All of the students in the school had been out there at one time or another, and all took turns planting flowers and keeping the grounds in order.

Sonny looked back at the lawmen and stared for a moment. They both stepped back a few more steps to give Sonny a bit of privacy.

Sonny looked down at the grave.

"This is the first time I've been out here to your grave, kid. I did my best to save you." His chest felt tight. "I've been staying in the storeroom where you stayed at the school. I'm using your reader too." He felt a tear escape his right eye. He shook his head and went on.

"It was hard at first, but it's getting easier all the time. I'm reading and writing real well now. Sara and Mrs. Donovan have helped me with my lessons. They're both real good teachers. I've been working over at the hospital with Dr. Jensen for my keep. They've fed me over there real well. He's a great man, Dr. Jensen. He's given me a chance in life, something my own father never did. Dr. Jensen told me he'd try to help me get into a fine medical college someday. Maybe it will happen, if I can get myself out of this mess. I think I'd like to deliver a lot of babies, maybe in a big hospital." Sonny felt his legs fall asleep, and shifted his weight to his knees.

"I know you're at peace now along with your folks. There haven't been any field trips since your accident. I'll honor your name by becoming the best doctor that I can, Jeb. I've got to go back to Virginia today. I have to stand trial for a murder I didn't commit."

Sonny took a pencil from behind his ear and wrote in the sandy dirt:

Nathan Jeb Wilson
1860–1873

He stood up and slowly walked into the bright morning sun. Sheriff Kelly and the deputy joined him as they headed for the train station. The deputy had all of the paperwork in a leather bag. As they climbed on to the train, the deputy handcuffed Sonny to the arm of the train seat.

"Sorry for this, Sonny. It's just procedure, ya know."

━━━━━━━━━━━━━━━

The train ride to Richmond, Virginia, where the trial would take place, took forever. The deputy stayed with Sonny until he was turned over to the authorities there. Sonny was exhausted from the trip. Both of his wrists were raw from wearing handcuffs the entire way. He had gotten little sleep. He tried reading a bit, but he missed

Sara and Mrs. Donovan, who would have helped him with the words he didn't know yet. When he arrived in the Richmond jail, he was immediately taken to a cell.

He was assigned a lawyer, Ada Kepley, a woman. She told him she would represent him in the trial because no other lawyer would touch the case, being that the bartender that was shot just happened to be the brother of the district judge in Virginia at the time.

"Are women allowed to be lawyers?"

Miss Kepley did not respond.

Hours went by, and as tired as he was from the trip across the country, Sonny told his side of the story to her.

"Sonny, I can't imagine that you would kill anybody. I believe you. But I have to say, I've talked to the little boy, and he tells it differently. He says you did it."

"You believe my story?"

"Yes, Sonny."

"That kid was just little. He was too scared to have thought straight."

"But he's pretty convincing."

"Have you found that old doctor yet? He'll tell you what really happened."

She shook her head. "Sorry. He's just plain missing."

"Are we gonna win?"

"I hope," she said, but he wasn't very assured.

A week later, court was in session. The crowd was frantic. They actually booed when Sonny was brought in. He wanted to shrink into the woodwork. How could he convince them that he didn't do it?

Sonny's heart leapt when he saw Mrs. Donovan and Dr. Jensen in the crowd. He couldn't believe they were there. They waved and smiled in the midst of the crowd of hisses.

The boy was placed on the stand to testify. It was damning. "I saw the man when he got shot," he said.

"Who did it?" asked the prosecutor.

The boy pointed to Sonny. The courtroom turned into a frenzy as the people there yelled curses at Sonny.

"I'm done for," thought Sonny.

The judge asked if there were any more witnesses.

Miss Kepley said, "No, your honor."

Suddenly, the doors in the back of the courtroom jumped open, and someone yelled, "Wait!"

In that instant, the whole room hushed. Everyone looked to the back. There, entering the courtroom were two men. A tall, middle-aged man in a dark suit pushed an old man in a wheelchair.

"There's another witness," yelled the middle-aged man. Sonny couldn't believe his eyes. He instantly recognized both men. Sonny smiled for the first time in days.

Sonny yelled out, "Pa?"

Sonny's pa shot a quick glance in Sonny's direction and smiled. "This man is the missing doctor," Sonny's father said to the judge. "He's been my patient. I didn't know who he was until he woke up from his coma."

Newspaper reporters ran out to file their scoops. After hearing the doctor's story, the judge dismissed the case. Sonny was free. He ran to the arms of Mrs. Donovan and Dr. Jensen.

Then he turned.

"Hello, son."

"Pa, what are you doing here?"

"I live here, remember?"

"Oh. Yeah."

"Sonny, when you left, I suddenly realized that something went wrong. I guess I was so wrapped up in being a doctor that I forgot to be a father." There was a long pause as his father looked over at Dr. Jensen. "You know, Sonny, Pete Jensen was a classmate of mine. He's written to me. I have known where you've been for months now. He came to see me when he arrived here a couple of days ago."

"By coincidence, old Doc Stanton, from Lynchburg was here in

Richmond for a seminar when he had a stroke. I had been treating him when he gradually came out of his coma. He had a lot to say." Sonny and his pa embraced.

His father continued. "I heard about what you did for the boy that died. And Dr. Jensen and Mrs. Donovan have told me about all your progress in school and at the hospital."

Sonny was never happier to see his father, a stranger of sorts.

"Do you think I could ever make it in medicine?"

"Sonny, you can make it in anything. I've taken the liberty of talking to a few contacts and have been promised you can have a position in the next class at the University of Pennsylvania School of Medicine, if you're interested."

Sonny looked at Dr. Jensen. Dr. Jensen smiled and nodded his head. Sonny looked back at his father.

"Yes, sir, I'm interested."

They all watched as the courtroom slowly cleared. Sonny reached into his pocket, pulled out his watch, opened it, and took a long look at his father's picture. His future was suddenly brighter.

———————

It was July 1881, on a busy street in downtown Philadelphia. There was a faint breeze blowing past the sign that hung over the red brick building. The sign read:

John Thomas Barlow, M.D.

Physician

Sonny Barlow, M.D.

Obstetrics

Sonny sat inside at a big desk in the medical office. In between patients, he was engaged in one of his favorite pastimes, reading the newspaper. He came across an article that was so intriguing that he had to read it twice to actually believe the words. The headlines read:

Henry McCarty, alias Kid Antrim, alias William H. Bonney, alias *Billy The Kid* was shot dead at Fort Sumner, New Mexico by Sheriff Pat Garrett.

Sonny jumped up out of his big leather chair and headed for his father's office next to his.

"Pa . . . Pa, you're never going to believe this . . . "

─────────────────

Author's Note

The Tale of Sonny Barlow began in Treasure Hill, Nevada in 1873. Actually, *The Tale of Sonny Barlow* began in 1981 in Hollywood, California. That's where I wrote the script for the TV Series, *Father Murphy*, starring Merlin Olsen and Katherine Cannon. Michael Landon created *Father Murphy* toward the end of *Little House On The Prairie*. As I developed the script into this juvenile fiction, the concept and story line remained the same, but many of the characters needed to be changed. One remained, however, and that's Moses. The part of Moses Gage in the TV series was really Moses Gunn in real life. He had worked with the Landon group as several different characters over the years and had always played very memorable parts. He was a friend and a fine actor and taught me a lot about acting and storytelling.

There are other characters in the book that are worth a note. One is Henry McCarty. And, according to Western folk lore, Henry McCarty was indeed Billy The Kid's birth name. The information about him is true to the best of my research. In 1873, the kid spent time in Silver City, New Mexico and the information about his mother is documented as well. Catherine McCarty died of galloping consumption in 1874.

Treasure Hill, Nevada did exist. Silver was discovered there in 1867. It was the home of the famous Hidden Treasure Silver Mine. Since the discovery of the silver mine, the little town grew at a steady pace. There were about 6000 people who lived there. The town was a collection of general stores, saloons, banks, blacksmith shops, and stables; there was also a theatre, ice cream parlor, and a hospital. Treasure Hill, smack dab in the middle of the Old West, was unusually cosmopolitan.

There was a Piaute Indian by the name of Napias Jim who helped to discover the Hidden Treasure Mine. *Napias* is an Indian word for silver. I named the Napias City School after this event.

And, Ada Kepley did exist. Although the events in this story are fictitious, she was really the first woman to graduate from a law school in the United States. She graduated from the Union College of Law in Chicago in 1870.

Sonny Barlow and the rest of the characters and events in The Tale of Sonny Barlow are all fiction.

THE TIRE BABY

Chapter 1

M eet Jimmy Chang.

This story is not about him, although he is in a lot of it. He is the estate manager, limousine driver, chef, maintenance man, and anything else needed for a very wealthy lady in Hong Kong. The lady's name is Mrs. Young, Cleopatra Young. She was born in Hong Kong and has lived here all of her life. No one really knows how she got that name.

There was a Mr. Young. He passed many years ago. Actually, it is presumed that he was murdered. The case was never solved.

The Youngs have a daughter. A beautiful, bright daughter who has studied abroad with a major in International Marketing in hopes of becoming a marketing executive. This story is not about her, either. Her name is Camille Zheng. She is twenty-two years old. She is tall and lean and has the most beautiful porcelain-doll skin you ever saw. She was basically raised by a nanny in the very mansion that Jimmy manages. She is very proper, beyond proper, in fact. But she can be a bit full of herself. She is returning to Hong Kong from the United States. She is bringing her college roommate with her. Both girls intend to work for Mrs. Young.

This story is about the roommate.

Her name is Nina Ramirez.

The Tire Baby.

More on that later.

Nina is also twenty-two, with long, jet-black hair. She is quite beautiful. No makeup and no pretenses. She wears jeans with a hole in the knee, sunglasses on the top of her head, and a beat-up leather purse slung over one shoulder.

So, the story begins with the girls arriving in Hong Kong. Jimmy is driving them from the airport in Mrs. Young's limousine. He looks in the mirror to see Nina thoroughly enjoying the lap of luxury. He sees Camille, with a scowl on her face, checking her makeup in a small compact mirror. She knows where they are going and she knows why, so she is not happy.

The limo arrives at the pier and Jimmy pulls over by one of the docks. Nina puts the window down and sees the fishermen's boats for the first time. There are happy screams from some of the children on the boats and laughter from children on others. There is smoke coming from several of the stoves that are on the decks of the boats, and women tending those stoves. Nina watches the everyday lives of the fishermen and their families.

Nina doesn't wait for Jimmy to come around the car; she opens the door and jumps out. Camille begins to get out. Jimmy offers her a hand. The disgusted look on her face defines her attitude regarding this whole situation.

"May I help you, Miss Camille?"

"Yes, thank you, Jimmy."

Jimmy pulls up the handle on the Louis Vuitton overnight bag on wheels, for Camille. Nina reaches into the trunk of the limo and grabs her canvas overnight bag. She heaves it on to her shoulder and begins to walk onto the jetty.

"The *Tigress* is the last one on the right, Miss Camille."

Camille manages a nod to Jimmy as she follows her roommate. After a couple of steps, Camille pulls a silk handkerchief out of her purse and covers her nose and mouth. Nina turns and sees Camille with the hanky.

"You crack me up, Camille."

The girls continue down the jetty to the last boat on the right, as Jimmy said. Nina spots the gold embossed letters on the transom that spell out *The Royal Tigress*.

"Wow. It didn't look this big from the car."

Tommy jumps up out of the deck chair he is relaxed in, on the aft deck of the *Tigress* when he hears the girls approaching. Camille looks around.

"She must be kidding."

"Camille, I don't think she is."

Tommy extends a hand to Camille to help her aboard.

"You must be Camille."

"Yes, Camille Zheng."

Nina climbs onto the deck and gives Tommy a hearty handshake.

"Hi. I'm Nina."

"Hi." Tommy takes an immediate interest in Nina.

"Ah . . . I'm Tommy Lee. I'm supposed to show you guys around." He looks at Camille. "I . . . ah . . . work for your mom."

Nina gives Tommy a big smile. "Tommy Lee, you mean, like the drummer?"

"Ah, no. No relation. Anyway, Mrs. Young wanted me to hang out until you get settled."

"There's no need for you to *hang out*. Nina and I are capable of finding our way around."

"Okay then. Down below are the guest quarters, bathrooms, galley, everything you need for the next few days."

Camille is quite familiar with the boat. "Yes, thank you, Tommy."

Tommy exits the boat. He offers a respectful nod to Camille and a big grin to Nina. He is halfway up the jetty when he passes two Hong Kong Security Bureau officers in uniform, heading for the *Tigress*. He turns and watches the officers. They climb down onto the boat. Tommy sees them talking. Camille reaches for her purse, digs out her ID and hands it to one of the two gentlemen. They look at it for a moment. Then, they focus their attention on Nina. She also rummages in her canvas bag for her ID and eventually surrenders it to the officers. There is some head shaking and shoulder shrugging. One officer climbs onto the dock, followed by the two girls, then by the second officer.

They walk down the dock to a waiting car. The car has a uniformed driver with several antennas on the roof.

Tommy sees the car speed away and he takes off running.

Chapter 2

The girls are escorted into an interview room at Police Central. They can see out of a large window into an outer office where several people are gathering.

"See the guy in the red tie? That's my mom's main lawyer."

"Camille, I'm not sure what we did wrong."

"We didn't do anything wrong, Nina. The officers said that some paperwork was missing when we came into the country."

Well, maybe for me, but you, you live here, Camille."

A few more men in suits come into the outer office. They are talking and pointing into the interview room. The cops have papers they are showing to the lawyers and the lawyers have papers they are showing the cops. The scene is not one of chaos, but it is one of confusion.

Nick Han, the Italian silk suit-wearing, well-coiffed attorney, is the head of Mrs. Young's legal team. He enters and is pointing at papers and talking and directing others who are coming and going. He seems to have everything under control.

He sticks his head in the room where the girls are. "Just a little mix up in the paperwork. I'll have you out of here in no time."

Chapter 3

The heavy cell door slams shut with a clunk. The girls are on the other side. The cell is grimy and dark. Camille pulls her hanky out of her sleeve and holds it over her nose. Camille and Nina can see through a small window in the steel door, into an entry room. Mr. Han is there with several guards. The guards unlock the door and let him into the cell area. He walks up to the cell where Camille is standing.

Camille glares at Mr. Han. "I thought you were going to get us out of here."

"Look, Camille, it's a little more complicated than we thought. You might have to stay in here tonight until I can get this all sorted out."

Camille pulls the hanky away from her nose. "What do you mean, tonight?"

"I'll do the best I can, Camille."

"If I'm not mistaken, Nick, my mother pays you a very handsome salary to prevent situations like this from happening in the first place."

Mr. Han nods to the guard to unlock the steel door so he can exit.

The cell is crowded with several women seated on a bunk attached to the wall. There is no mattress. Nina sits on the second bunk. She is quiet.

Two of the women sit on either side of Nina. Nina attempts to get up. One of the women stands in front of her. The woman has a long scar on her right cheek and burn marks on both arms.

Two other women approach Camille. One begins to stroke Camille's hair. The other one rubs the back of her finger along Camille's porcelain-doll cheek.

Camille resists. She pushes the woman's hand out of the way. "Stop it, Leave me alone."

Several of the women surround Camille. One of the inmates grabs her by the hair and pushes her face into the cold steel bars.

Camille pushes the inmate out of the way, "I said leave me *alone*. Stop touching me."

A second inmate grabs Camille from the back and covers her mouth. A struggle begins with Camille and several of the women.

Nina gets up from the bunk she is on and attempts to help Camille but is pushed to the floor. Nina gets up and shouts for help.

One of the women slaps Nina across the face.

The struggle continues.

Nina holds her hand on her cheek as she tries to see what is happening to her friend.

One of the inmates produces a plastic knife-like object from her sleeve.

She lunges towards Camille and thrusts the object deep into Camille's chest.

A second thrust.

A twist.

A hand covers Camille's mouth.

Not a sound is made.

Camille's lifeless body drops to the floor.

There is a trickle of blood finding its way to the drain in the floor.

Then, there is a stream of blood.

Chapter 4

Mrs. Young is ailing from a pulmonary disease. She is propped up in her king-sized bed on several pillows in a very large bedroom. There is a fireplace, a sofa and several stuffed chairs, a desk with nothing on it, and a sofa table cluttered with prescription bottles and a cup of steaming tea.

Mrs. Young is a petite woman and wears a Hawaiian muumuu. Maggie finishes up with Mrs. Young's breathing treatment and hangs the oxygen mask over the top of the tank. Maggie, an American nurse, has worked for Mrs. Young exclusively for more than twenty years. She helps Mrs. Young to stand.

"Maggie, help me over to my favorite chair. I'll wait for Nina there."

The chair is old and worn and out of place in Mrs. Young's perfectly designed room.

"Here, ma'am. Your tea is ready for you."

As she is seated there is a knock at the door.

"It's Nina. Show her in, Maggie."

Maggie opens the door. Mrs. Young's eyes widen.

"Oh, it's you."

Tommy enters the room. He is a bit surprised at her attitude.

"I was expecting Nina."

"Jimmy is bringing her up now, ma'am."

"Okay, thank you, Tommy."

"Anything else, Mrs. Young?"

"No, no. That's all for now, Tommy."

As Tommy exits, Nina enters smiling. Mrs. Young struggles a bit to get to her feet. "It's good to see you up and around, Nina." Maggie rushes over to her aid but is brushed off. Mrs. Young gives Nina a big hug.

"Sit, sit." Mrs. Young sits again. She gives a long look at Nina. "So?"

Nina's eyes begin to fill with tears.

"I can only cry and sleep for so long. And, everyone here has been so nice."

"Well, maybe we can change that." Mrs. Young takes a couple sips of her tea. "Would you care for some tea, dear?"

"No, thanks." Nina grabs a tissue from the Kleenex box on the table. She wipes at her eyes.

Mrs. Young shows little emotion.

"Nina, you and Camille were supposed to stay on the yacht and observe a family on a fishing boat for a very good reason."

"We weren't on the yacht long enough to find out."

"I know, dear. Camille and I were about to launch a philanthropic mission."

Nina sits back in the big stuffed chair.

"You see, Camille may not have talked about it much at school, but our Tigress perfume business has been very successful, internationally, and has netted a substantial profit."

Maggie takes that as a cue to leave. "Will there be anything else, ma'am?"

"No Maggie, thank you."

The room is silent while Maggie leaves the room. When the big oak door closes, Mrs. Young continues. "I had planned to give away a large portion of our fortune and make life easier for people who need it."

"Well, how does that affect me, Mrs. Young?"
"Nina, I would like you to stay on here and help me with this project."

"I would give away your money?"

"That's right dear. One million dollars at a time."

Chapter 5

Wein Hall is on the east side of the Columbia University campus. It's a beautiful brick building dating back to 1925. It houses undergraduate students. Students are milling around the big arch entrance in front, some entering and some leaving.

Alex is twenty-five, tall, and thin. He wears a hoodie, shades, and backwards ball cap with the interlocking NY above the bill.

He looks up at the arch and enters.

Officer Steele sits at the front desk. He is a seasoned officer of the public safety department and sees Alex enter, eyes shifting back and forth as if he were lost.

"ID, please."

Alex leans on the front desk very confidently.

"Well, I'm not actually a student here. I'm looking for a girl."

"Aren't they all?" Officer Steele looks over the top of his reading glasses. "Sorry, but I can't let you past this point without a valid ID."

"Maybe you know her. Her name is Nina Ramirez."

"Look kid, there are over thirteen thousand girls on this campus, it's hard to remember all their names." Officer Steele softens, "Try Hamilton Hall on the main campus. That's the Dean's office. They should know where to find her."

Alex enters Hamilton Hall with confidence and a few minutes later exits with his head down. He heads over to the Public Safety office in Low Library. Again, he leaves shaking his head. He has one more place to try. He walks in the direction of Lerner Hall where the University Chaplain's office is.

After a short time, he exits with a smirk on his face. He flags down a cab on the corner of 114th and Broadway.

As he gets into the cab, Alex leans forward in the plexiglass window, "JFK, please."

Chapter 6

Mrs. Young sits on the edge of her big king-sized bed. She is watching *The Millionaire*, a black and white 1950s television series, on her sixty-five-inch plasma screen.
She begins to cough.
She takes a hit of her inhaler and continues to cough.
She manages to reach the intercom on her bedside table.
She pushes the button and holds it down.
"Maggie, Maggie!"
Maggie races into the room.
She grabs the phone and calls an ambulance.

Chapter 7

The Tai Po Hospital Emergency Room is relatively quiet. There are a few doctors and nurses seated behind the big desk eating pizza and having a discussion.

The stretcher comes bursting through the double glass doors with a loud thud. Mrs. Young is lying on the stretcher with an oxygen mask in place.

Her color is ashen.

She has IVs running and the plastic bags swing on their poles as the EMTs make their way into the treatment room.

There are several workers in white lab coats buzzing in and out of the treatment room. One of the nurses pulls the privacy curtain around Mrs. Young's bed.

Dr. Chung comes out from behind the curtain. She is calm, but assertive. She hands a chart to one of the clerks behind the desk, "Are there any family members waiting?"

Both of the girls behind the desk shake their heads no.

"Alright, see if you can locate the next of kin. If you can, have them come in as soon as possible."

Dr. Chung walks back in the room where Mrs. Young is being treated. As she disappears behind the privacy curtain, Nina comes into the Emergency Department, disheveled, crying, and lost.

"They just brought in my friend, Mrs. Young."

One of the girls looks at the chart and then up at Nina. "Are you a family member?"

"No, but I work for Mrs. Young. Is she going to be alright?"

"Your name, Miss?"

Nina is a little unnerved. "Nina, Nina Ramirez."

"You can wait in the conference room, right through those double doors. I will let Dr. Chung know that you are here."

Nina goes into the conference room and takes a seat at the end of a long table.

She sits facing the door.

Her eyes flash from the clock to the door.

She watches the commotion outside the conference room.

The short, but very pretty lady in a long white coat enters and closes the door slowly behind her.

"You're Nina? Mrs. Young's daughter?"

"No . . . I'm Nina Ramirez, a close friend of the family."

"Does Mrs. Young have any family, Nina?"

"No, not anymore, but I work for her now."

Dr. Chung sits opposite Nina, "Well, I'm Dr. Chung. I took care of Mrs. Young when she came in today."

Dr. Chung gets right to business, "Nina, Mrs. Young had a fairly acute episode this time. She has been in here many times before today with the same problem. As you may know, the disease process is slowly taking away her capacity to breathe."

Nina listens intently.

Dr. Chung continues, "We were able to get her back breathing on her own pretty quickly this time."

"When will she be able to go home?"

"You can take her home tomorrow morning, if she keeps improving."

Nina shows a look of relief.

"You know, Nina, this isn't going to get better."

Chapter 8

Seated at the table in the kitchen of the mansion are Mrs. Young and Nina. Mrs. Young is smiling, pink in color, and appears much improved from the day before. Jimmy clears the plates.

"Will there be anything else, ma'am?"

"No, thank you, Jimmy. The omelet was quite good today."

Jimmy nods and smiles, "Anything else for you, Miss Nina?"

Nina shakes her head no but lifts her empty coffee cup.

Jimmy scowls at Tommy, "Tommy. Coffee."

Tommy grabs the coffee pot and walks over to the table. He fills Mrs. Young's cup first. Mrs. Young lifts the tea bag from her cup and offers raised eyebrows to Tommy. Tommy begins to fill Nina's cup as he catches a glimpse of her low cut shirt and he overfills the cup. Coffee now runs on the top of the table as Jimmy races for the towels.

Mrs. Young attempts to ease the situation, "My, Tommy, you

certainly have been spending a lot of time in the house the last couple of days. What is it that seems to need all of this attention?"

Tommy gives the table a final wipe with the towel. "Actually, ma'am, I was just trying to help Miss Nina get settled."

"Now that you mention it, Tommy, I need you to take Nina out to the yacht later today so she can observe a family by the name of Lau. They work a fishing boat and they may be the first recipient of the money."

Mrs. Young and Nina get up and start to leave the kitchen.

"Oh, Tommy. I want you to stay with Nina today while she is on the yacht. Nina, you can fill me in at dinner with the observations you have made."

Jimmy rolls his eyes at Tommy, "You'll still be riding with me in the front seat on the way there."

After they arrive, Tommy assists Nina aboard and they find a couple of deck chairs. They face the Lau's fishing boat. Nina has a legal pad and a pen. Tommy stares at Nina.

Chapter 9

Alex makes his way through a busy JFK Airport. He spots the Air China ticket counter. He is the only one in line and approaches the agent.

"I need a one way ticket to Hong Kong, please."

"On what flight, sir?"

"Well, the next available."

"There's a flight that leaves in about five hours. A standby ticket will be five hundred fifty-seven dollars and sixty-two cents."

"Standby? How do you know I don't want to travel first class?"

Clearly embarrassed, the ticket agent stammers, "Well, I just thought . . . that. . ."

"Okay. I'll take the standby ticket."

Alex begins to count out cash. The agent becomes suspicious and nods at a TSA officer who is standing close by.

"Do you have luggage to check, sir?"

"No, I'll just carry on my backpack."

"Aren't you traveling a little light for a trip to China?"

Alex replies, very matter-of-factly, "No. I don't plan on being there that long."

Alex proceeds to the screening area, with the eyes of several TSA officers on him.

Backpack in the plastic bin.

Shoes off and in the plastic bin.

Cell phone, keys, and change in the plastic bin.

Alex passes through the magnetometer.

The alarm sounds.

The TSA officer motions for Alex to stand still.

"Right over this way, sir."

The TSA officer has Alex hold his arms out as he waves the wand over his shoulders and down the front of his shirt. As the officer passes the wand by Alex's belt the alarm is activated.

A second TSA officer responds by coming into the secluded area where Alex is standing.

"Shirt up, please sir."

Alex raises his shirttail above his belt to reveal a large metal buckle. The buckle has a gold eagle with a snake in its mouth.

"Could I see your ticket and passport, please?"

The TSA officer takes a long look at the ticket and then holds the passport picture up next to Alex's face. He offers the documents to the second officer. The second officer takes a look at them and hands them back to Alex. "Have a nice flight, sir, You're free to go."

Hours pass.

Alex is seated in the waiting area as the chairs begin to fill up. When the time approaches for boarding, he heads for the standby line. There are two attractive girls about his age in front of him. He listens to their conversation. They are laughing and using *like* at least four times in every sentence. Finally, the group is called and they start walking toward the jet way.

The ticket agent holds out his hand. "May I see your ticket, please?"

Alex hands the agent his ticket.

"Coach is full, but we have one seat left in first class, if you would be willing to take it."

"Willing to take it?" Alex does a double take. "Yeah, I'd be willing to take it."

The agent points to the jet way.

"Right that way sir."

Alex steps forward and turns back to the agent, "This is for the same price, right?"

The agent smiles and shakes his head yes.

Alex enters the plane in the forward coach section. He spots the two girls and takes the aisle seat next to them. They smile at one another and continue their conversation. The flight attendant sees Alex and asks to see his ticket.

"Oh, sir, you're in first class, right up there. This is coach."

The two girls stop their conversation and offer looks of surprise.

Alex turns to the girls, hesitates for a second, "I'm sorry. I'm *like* in first class."

Chapter 10

Mrs. Young and Nina sit in the elegant dining room of the mansion. They are at opposite ends of a twenty-foot dining table. The table has been set with the finest silver and crystal. Nina stares at all of the silverware.

She takes her gum out of her mouth but isn't sure what to do with it. She holds the gum with one hand and opens the fine linen napkin with the other. She puts the gum back in her mouth and swallows it.

The salad has been served.

She picks up the dinner fork.

A waiter, Tio, looks at her and simply points to the salad fork. She picks up the salad fork.

"Mrs. Young?"

"Yes, Nina?"

"Could I move down there with you?" Nina cups her hands around her mouth. "I feel as though I have to shout."

Mrs. Young motions to Tio to move her place setting.

"Of course, dear. Please join me."

Tio and one of the maids see what is happening and they rush to Nina's aid, moving her silver and plates near Mrs. Young.

Nina sits, smiles, and is immediately more comfortable.

She is now ready to enjoy her salad, except Tio has put the forks back in order again.

Mrs. Young points to the salad fork, "That one."

Both women take a few bites of salad.

"Nina, what did you learn today?"

"You mean at the docks?"

Mrs. Young smiles. "Yes, you and Tommy were watching the Lau family."

Nina begins to cry, "I'm sorry, Mrs. Young." She wipes her eyes with the linen napkin.

"I know it's sometimes sad to watch, Nina, but that's all they know, dear. That's the only life they've ever had."

"No, not them. . . Camille. I miss Camille."

Mrs. Young pauses for a moment, "So do I, dear. But we'll recover and we'll both be fine. I've got you now."

Chapter 11

Alex sits in his first-class seat on the aisle. He is clearly enjoying his standby ride. He pulls his backpack out from underneath the seat in front of him. He rummages through the pack for a moment. He pulls an eight-by-ten picture out of an old, tattered envelope.

The photo is worn, sepia in tone with one corner torn off.

He stares at it for a bit, then puts it back in the envelope. He holds the envelope close to his chest. He leans the big leather seat back and he drifts off to sleep.

It is a very hot Texas afternoon at the South Laredo Border Station. Captain Rojas and Officer Macias are watching the monitors at the big video console in the station's main room. Macias sees some action and calls the captain over to the monitor.

"Hey, Cap. Look at number six. Looks like we got a live one on the river."

The captain studies the monitor for a minute, "Okay, get Hernandez in Unit Four over there right away. He's only about a half mile from there."

"Copy that."

A large tractor tire is floating on the river. There is a lady and a young boy riding on the top of it. A coyote, a paid smuggler, who helps immigrants cross the border, pulls the big tire with a rope toward the American shore. Another man holds the back of the tire. As the tire approaches the shore on the American side, the coyote pulls the tire up, into the sand with the rope. The coyote takes a package out of the tire and hands it to the lady.

The package is a baby.

The man in back of the tire spots a border patrol officer running in his direction. He points to the hills. The man grabs the young boy and they take off running up the bank. The coyote grabs the baby from the lady and the three of them run in another direction. "Corra! Corra!" Run! Run!

The border patrol officer catches up to the man and the boy. He wrestles the man to the ground.

The young boy doesn't move.

The officer handcuffs the man's wrist to the boy's wrist. In a few seconds, the boy pulls his little five year old wrist free and takes off running. The officer handcuffs the man around the tractor tire this time. He heads off to find the boy who has disappeared in the sand. The coyote with the baby and the lady have run out of sight.

The flight attendant leans over Alex and taps him on the shoulder.

"Sir? Sir? Sorry to wake you. Can you bring your seat to the upright position please? We will be landing in Hong Kong soon."

Chapter 12

Nina sits at the big dining room table. Jimmy enters and puts her breakfast down in front of her.

"Jimmy, this is silly."

"Ma'am?"

"Can I just eat in the kitchen? Why do I need to be here in this big room all by myself?

"As you wish, Miss Nina."

Jimmy gathers the place setting and the breakfast plate and follows Nina to the kitchen. Nina sees Tommy as he enters from a back door.

"Tommy, you're taking me out to the docks again this afternoon, right?"

"Yes, Miss Nina."

"Tommy, could you just call me, Nina?"

"Sure."

"Have some breakfast with me."

Jimmy gives a very disapproving look.

"C'mon. Sit here. I'd like some company. Besides, we're going to be working together for a while."

Jimmy snaps back, "Oh really? In what context?"

"In the context of me asking Mrs. Young if he can. I'm going to need help for a while and Tommy is the most logical candidate."

Jimmy is not convinced. "Perhaps."

"Jimmy, can you take us out to the docks later?" "Of course, Miss Nina. Tommy has a project to finish in Miss Camille's suite, but after that, I'd be happy to."

Chapter 13

Tommy is stacking boxes on a dolly with Jimmy managing his every move. They are in Camille's room. Camille's suite, rather.

Tommy heaves a heavy box of files on top of the pile, only to have it fall off, spilling all the files loaded with papers all over the floor.

Jimmy looks disgusted.

"After you're done cleaning all this up, bring the boxes down to the storage room.

Jimmy shakes his head.

"And this isn't the only thing we have to do before you go to the docks with Miss Nina."

Tommy starts to pick up the fallen papers, "Okay, okay. I'll be down in a little bit."

Jimmy leaves the room without another word. Tommy picks up a padded envelope with an open flap. There is another envelope inside. Inside the second envelope are some index cards bound tightly with a couple of rubber bands. He examines the cards. There is writing on them in Cantonese. On the top of the first card, in English, he reads, *Tigress.*

Jimmy looks around the suite, then puts the stack of cards in his pocket. He finishes his packing and begins to move the dolly out of the room. He grabs the door handle with one hand and manages a big fist pump with the other, "Yes. Tigress."

Chapter 14

Maggie stands besides Mrs. Young in her bedroom as she finishes her breathing treatment. Mrs. Young coughs a couple of times and then heads for her favorite chair. Maggie is very quiet.

"Okay, Maggie, what is it?"

"Ah, what is what, Mrs. Young?"

"Maggie, you've been with me for twenty years. I know when something is bothering you. Now what is it?"

Maggie pauses for a moment, "I don't trust her."

"You don't trust who, Maggie?"

"Nina, that's who."

"Well, why on earth not?"

"I don't know, ma'am. Just a feeling I have. Something she said or a look that she's given. I just have this funny feeling."

Mrs. Young lets that sink in.

"Maggie, I have taken Nina in as a partner in the perfume company and as a partner in the philanthropic work I've started." She gives a rather stern look to Maggie. "She was Camille's best friend and I've learned to love her like my own and in a very short time. Any other questions, Maggie?"

Maggie gets up to leave, "Yes ma'am. Would you care for some tea?"

Chapter 15

Jimmy is working away in the kitchen. Tommy and Nina are sitting at the bar, laughing like a couple of school kids.

"Jimmy, I think we're ready," Nina says.

"*We* are?"

"Yeah, me and Tommy. We're ready to tell Mrs. Young what we found out about the Lau family. If she's happy with the information, then we will be able to give them the first check."

Jimmy is not convinced that she and Tommy are ready for anything.

"Would you care for something to drink, Miss Nina?"

"Yes, I would love a ginger ale."

Jimmy looks in Tommy's direction.

"Tommy?" Jimmy motions to the refrigerator. "You still work here, don't you?"

Tommy gets up off the bar stool, goes to the refrigerator and produces two ginger ales.

He pops the tab for Nina and hands her the can.

He opens the other one for himself.

They take a couple of drinks.

Jimmy is looking up at the security monitors on the kitchen wall.

"Tommy, there's somebody out at the front gate. Would you go out and see who it is? But don't open the door."

Tommy leaves the kitchen right away.

Jimmy focuses on the TVs, "Are you expecting anyone, Miss Nina?"

"Not me."

"Well, we aren't either."

Jimmy leaves the kitchen and Nina follows him to the front door. They join Tommy.

"Some guy with a backpack."

Jimmy goes to the intercom, "May I help you?"

"Yes, I'm looking for a Nina Ramirez. I'm told that she lives here."

Jimmy pushes the talk button on the intercom again.

"Who may I ask is calling?"

There is silence.

"Hello . . . who's calling please?"

"It's . . . ah . . . Alex, a friend. I'd like to speak to Nina if I may."

Jimmy takes his finger off the talk button.

"Miss Nina, do you know anyone by that name?"

Nina doesn't have to think about it. "No, I'm afraid I don't. I don't know anybody by that name."

Jimmy turns to Nina, "Miss Nina, I think you'll find out that when you have a lot of money and live in a house like this, you suddenly have a lot of friends that you didn't realize you had."

The intercom buzzes again.

"Please sir, I've come all this way to see her."

"I'm sorry, young man, we can't help you."

"Uh sir, I brought this . . ."

Jimmy turns off the intercom.

Alex takes off the backpack as quickly as he can. He digs around in it to find the envelope he had on the plane. He pulls out the envelope. He takes out the eight-by-ten photo and holds it up to the camera by the iron gates.

Tommy and Nina start down the hallway back towards the kitchen.

Alex waits for a response, but there is none. He buzzes the intercom again, but there is no answer. He puts the old photo back into the envelope and slides it under the huge door.

Nina hears the envelope being jammed under the door and turns back to look. She goes back to pick up the envelope. She opens it and pulls out the eight-by-ten photo. Her eyes widen as she stares at it.

Chapter 16

The envelope lays on the big table in the study.

Nina and Alex sit on opposite sides of the table, both staring at the envelope.

Tommy paces back and forth in the back of the room.

Jimmy stands by the door.

Nina pulls the picture out of the envelope and takes a long look at it.

Finally, Nina speaks, "Where did you get this?"

Alex gives a look to Tommy and Jimmy.

Nina looks at Tommy, "I'll be okay here. We're just going to talk for a while."

Tommy gives Nina a look then directs his gaze to the security camera over the door.

Nina follows his look to the camera, "Yes, thank you, Tommy."

Tommy and Jimmy both exit leaving the door ajar.

Nina gets up from the table and goes to the door.

She closes it quietly.

She sits back down in the chair and stares at the picture again.

"I'm at a bit of a loss for words." Nina holds her focus on the picture. "Obviously, I have seen this picture before, but how is it that you have it? My mother showed it to me many years ago. I never did understand what was going on and she never bothered to explain it to me."

Alex points to the little boy in the picture.

"That's me, Nina. And, that's our father and that's our mother."

Nina looks deep into Alex's eyes. After a long pause she whispers, "You're my brother."

Chapter 17

Jimmy and Tommy are in the kitchen. Tommy is pacing around the service island.

"I'll bet that's her boyfriend. She never told us she had a boyfriend."

"Tommy, that may not be true. But whoever he is, it's none of our business."

"Well, she should have told us she had a boyfriend."

Chapter 18

Over an hour has passed and Nina and Alex are still seated in the study separated by the big table and the picture. The shock on both their faces has been replaced by smiles.

"And so, after I graduated from Burbank High School and then Columbia in New York, I came here with Camille. On our first night in country we ended up in jail. Camille was stabbed to death for no reason other than being beautiful and rich. Now, I live in a mansion, ride around in a limousine, and work for Mrs. Young. She owns a huge perfume business and has started a philanthropic organization to help those in need. She has asked me to stay and work for her."

"Well, what does that mean, exactly?"

"It means I basically give away her money for a living." Nina pauses for a moment. "I'm kinda new at it and I just lost my best friend, so I'm having a rough start." Nina picks up the picture, "So Alex, the picture."

"This is a picture that the border patrol took over twenty years ago. When I found our mother in Los Angeles, she gave it to me. The border patrol caught our father. He went to jail. I went to a foster home—several, in fact. You and Mama made it to Aunt Lidia's in South Central LA and then I lost track of everyone.

"I was a street kid. I failed in school—every school—but I managed to survive on the street. I was convinced that I could find a better life, so I started asking questions. I finally found Mama in Burbank working for a really nice family that has treated her very well."

Alex grabs his backpack and digs out a small picture to show his sister.

"Here, check this out. Me and Mama in front of the fireplace. Nina, she looks so old. And, she still only knows a few words in English. I don't know how she has survived all these years. That picture was taken about a month or so ago. When was the last time you talked to her?"

"It's been a while. My plan was to get settled and then bring her over here when I saved enough for the trip. That doesn't really seem to be a problem now. Camille was always very secretive about her situation, and now I know why. I mean, who would have believed her? Mansion. Limousine. Yacht. Perfume business."

"Okay, sis, what's your plan now?"

Nina thinks for a minute. "Well, the first thing we have to do is get you introduced to Mrs. Young, not to mention Tommy and Jimmy. They were about to have the security guards throw you out into the street. C'mon, let's go see Mrs. Young."

Nina and Alex head up the steps to see Mrs. Young in her bedroom. Tommy is already there, nervously pacing outside of Mrs. Young's bedroom door.

Tommy stops Alex on the top step.

"So, are you her boyfriend?"

"Boyfriend? No, I'm Nina's brother."

Tommy raises both eyebrows. "Brother? Are you sure?"

Alex is befuddled. "Am I sure? . . . Yes, I'm quite sure. Are you her boyfriend?"

"No. I'm her ah . . . her . . . we both work for Mrs. Young."

The big oak bedroom door swings open. Maggie invites Nina, Tommy, and Alex in to speak with Mrs. Young.

Chapter 19

The noon sun shines brightly on the Beverly Hills Office Suite in downtown Hong Kong. Mrs. Young enters the big conference room where Nina, Tommy, and Alex are casually seated.

She sits in one of the leather swivel chairs. The room is rather spartan in design. She looks at Alex.

"Well, after our meeting last night at the house, I was very impressed with your story, and impressed with your dedication to find your sister and reunite your family. This morning Mr. Han finished his investigation and you seem to be who you say you are. Alex, I'm happy to invite you into our organization and hope you will stay on to work with Nina. I'd like you to stay with Nina and Tommy while they present the gift to the Lau family. Jimmy will take me back to the house now, while you get ready for the presentation. Let me know how it goes."

As Jimmy escorts Mrs. Young out one door, Tommy brings the Lau family in the conference room. Nina is on one side of the table. Alex sits beside her. Tommy offers the six family members chairs on the opposite side.

They take their time looking around the room, all muttering to each other.

Nina reads from an index card, "Mr. Lau and family."

Tommy translates to Cantonese simultaneously as Nina continues to read, "The reason you were invited here today was to announce to you that you have been chosen to receive a large sum of money to be used at your discretion."

The Laus all look at one another. They aren't clear what Nina is saying.

Tommy gets up and moves to the other side of the table closer to the Laus. He explains to them that they are not permitted to reveal the amount of the gift or the identity of the benefactor.

Nina hands Mr. Lau the form to sign and he gets up to leave. Tommy quickly asks Mr. Lau to be seated again, explaining that the form is not the check.

Nina hands the check to Tommy, who, in turn, hands it to Mr. Lau. He shows it to all of the relatives.

They are all shocked.

One cries.

A couple of them look around, not sure what has just happened.

Then, there is a discussion among the family members.

Tommy translates to English for Nina and Alex.

"The Laus would like to know your name. They want to buy a new fishing boat and name it after you."

"That's very nice but please explain to Mr. Lau that we cannot give out our names due to the conditions of the gift; instead they should consider calling the new boat Camille."

Chapter 20

The Emergency Room at Tai Po Hospital is very busy. Mrs. Young is in Treatment Room 1, unconscious. A plethora of tubes hang from the IV poles. Monitors beep as Nina stands by the bedside holding Mrs. Young's hand. Dr. Chung enters, looks at the monitors, then looks at Nina. A tear rolls down Nina's face, "Dr. Chung, is she going to be alright?"

Chapter 21

The graveside service has ended and Jimmy leads Nina, along with Tommy and Alex back to the limousine. It is a silent ride back to the mansion. A few looks are exchanged. Nina wipes tears from her eyes.

A very stoic Nina looks at the boys.

"Okay, so we meet with Mr. Han tomorrow in the office and find out where we go from here."

Chapter 22

The driving rain pelts the glass walls of the Beverly Hills office suite. Nick Han sits at the head of the conference table; Nina, Tommy, and Alex sit on one side, Jimmy on the other.

"I'm sure I don't have to tell you that the last couple of weeks have been extraordinary. I had met with Mrs. Young several times recently to change her will to reflect all the changes in her life, the life of Tigress and the future of the philanthropy."

Mr. Han passes out copies of the documents for the foursome to read.

"I will summarize the main points of the will for you. You can read it in detail when you have time, but this is what she wanted.

"Maggie will be generously taken care of in her retirement. Jimmy, you will get the mansion that you have taken care of all these years and the limousine. You are free to do with them what you please.

"Nina, you are the only beneficiary of the Tigress Perfume business. It has been very kind to Mrs. Young and she hoped that you would continue to run the business and let it generate funds to be used by the philanthropy that she set up. She further hopes that your two associates here will continue to work with you in distributing the trust that is worth upwards of four hundred million dollars."

Jimmy smiles and nods. The others are shocked. Nina looks at Mr. Han. She mouths in silence, "Four hundred million?"

"That's right, Nina, four hundred million."

Mr. Han continues, "Now regarding the business. You know how she would not embrace technology."

Nina shakes her head, "I know. She hated computers, didn't trust them and wouldn't go near them. Everything was written on scraps of paper or legal pads."

Mr. Han agrees, "Having said that, unfortunately, the formula for Tigress is written somewhere and is filed or stored somewhere in this office or somewhere in the mansion. Only Camille knew where it was kept. The future of the business depends on finding that formula. So, you three have your work cut out for you. Please contact me if you have any questions, I know this is a lot to digest right now."

"Unfortunately, the formula for Tigress is distributed among many departments, so only one person knows their part of the formula, and Camille knew where the composite formula was kept. Sorta like Coca-Cola and KFC. Somewhere in the house is the composite formula. The trick will be to find it. That formula will be key to continuing the production of the perfume.

Mr. Han stands and jams some papers in his briefcase.

"I'm sure after you have digested all this, you will have questions. I will be available anytime. Jimmy, can you drive me back to my office?"

"Of course, Mr. Han."

Jimmy looks at the threesome.

"I'll see you all tonight for dinner?"

Nina shakes her head, "Yes, but tonight let's eat in the dining room, with the salad forks and everything, okay?"

Jimmy nods and smiles. "Okay. See you tonight."

Jimmy exits with Mr. Han.

Tommy looks at Nina.

"Nina, could I see you and Alex for a minute?" Tommy gestures to Nina and Alex to be seated. He pulls the index cards out of his pocket and shows them to Nina. "I found these when I was cleaning out Miss Camille's suite. I do believe this is what Mr. Han was talking about."

Nina takes the cards and looks at them carefully, passing some to Alex and then handing them all back to Tommy.

"Let's get those digitized and on a hard drive and locked up safe somewhere. Somewhere that only the three of us know. Tommy?"

"I can see to that."

"While you two work on that, I have someplace to go before dinner tonight."

Nina enters Mrs. Young's bedroom. There is a light on, on a table next to her favorite chair.

She walks around the room slowly.

She passes by the big bed.

She walks by the table with all the bottles of medicine on it.

She walks over to the fireplace.

She stops to look at a picture that sits on the mantle.

She squints a bit in the low light and then heads for Mrs. Young's favorite chair.

She sits in her chair and studies the picture in the frame. It's an old photograph of Mrs. Young and Camille by a fireplace.

Nina looks lovingly at the picture.

Tears run down her cheeks.

She stares at the mother and daughter and a big smile comes over her.

Chapter 23

The table is set with the best crystal and china.

Jimmy is at one end of the big dining room table.

Nina is at the other end.

Tommy and Alex are seated on the sides of the table, opposite each other.

Nina lifts her head. "I have been doing some thinking about where to go from here. I spent some time in Mrs. Young's bedroom earlier today and I was looking at a picture of a mother and daughter."

Jimmy is calm and relaxed. Tommy and Alex are excited to hear what she has to say.

"Wait a minute. This just isn't working."

Nina motions to the waiter.

"Tio, can you move the guys down here with me?"

Suddenly, there is commotion in the room, as the three men get up to move.

There are two maids that join in to help move the threesome closer to Nina.

All of the silver and crystal and china are moved as the three of them are gathered around Nina at her end of the table.

"Now, that's so much better."

Tommy and Alex are waiting for the answer of where things will go from here.

"I have decided to move the headquarters of Tigress perfume and Mrs. Young's philanthropic business to Los Angeles. That's where I grew up and there are a lot of people there that need help. There's a lady there in Burbank that could use some help and I want to find a man in Mexico and help him as well."

A big smile comes over Alex's face.

"Alex, I gather you will go and help me on this mission?" She turns to Tommy. "And Tommy, I hope you will come with us. I haven't really gotten to know you all that well, but I believe we work well together. I've never heard anything about your family or where you are from.

"I never talked about it much."

"Why not?"

"Mrs. Young took care of me pretty much my whole life. I got in trouble in school and she put me to work and gave me a purpose. I needed to work to help my family."

"How is your family doing now?"

"Oh, they're doing great."

Nina lifts her eyebrows. "How so?"

"Well, I changed my name to Lee. Thought if it were more Americanized, I would do better. Plus, I have always wanted to go to the States. I learned English and speak it very well."

"You do indeed speak it well, but what's that got to do with your family?"

"My name used to be Lau."

All eyes widen at this news.

"Well, that certainly answers a lot of questions."

"I would love to come to the States with you, Nina."

"It's settled then. Jimmy, can we stay here when we come back to Hong Kong for a visit?"

"Miss Nina, you are welcome here in my home, anytime."

Nina picks up her salad fork and shows it to everyone.

"Tio, we are ready for the salads."